PARROT
&SWEENEY

ALAN ROBERTS

ISBN: 0615353894
ISBN-13: 9780615353890

Murder of a Nobleman

Detective Chief Inspector George Parrot, known affectionately to colleagues, and not so affectionately to offenders, by the rather unimaginative and obvious nickname of 'Polly', was preparing to leave the station for home, via a swift pint at The Feathers, his local watering hole, when Sergeant Dan Sweeney suddenly appeared, wearing a look of consternation that Parrot knew only too well.

'And there was I, just this afternoon, thinking how unusually quiet it's been lately.' said Parrot, before continuing.

'Alright Sergeant what's happened?'

'We've just received a call from Headley Grange. Sir Arthur Messenger's been murdered. It sounds like a nasty business.'

'Okay Sweeney, it's not every day one of our leading dignitaries gets himself killed. Give me a couple of minutes to call my wife, then you can fill me in with the details on the way up there.'

During the short drive, Sweeney told his boss about the distressed phone call he had received from a Ms Gwen Silsbury, the Messenger's housekeeper. Between sobs, she had managed to relate that Sir Arthur had been murdered, and that his body had been discovered by the head gardener.

'You know, Sweeney, I met Sir Arthur many times, and a sweeter man never lived. Why anyone would think of harming the old boy is quite beyond me. But as for that wife of his, Lady Marjorie. That's quite another story. Her nose is so far up in the air, she only breathes mountain air,' Parrot said with his usual chuckle, following any attempt at his very own particular brand of humor.

Sweeney pulled into Headley Grange and began the half mile uphill climb to the castle, as it was known locally. Reaching the top, the two policemen were greeted with the imposing sight of the finest example of Georgian architecture in the county, set in seven hundred acres of sprawling English countryside at its finest, replete with rolling hills, dense areas of woodland, a natural lake and a bird sanctuary.

'Wow,' said Sweeney. 'Just look at the size of this place. A bit big just for the Messengers, don't you think, Sir?'

'You obviously don't keep in touch with local events, Sergeant. Part of the castle is open to the public. Sir Arthur and his family live in one of the wings and there is of course an area designated for his students.'

'Students, Sir?' Sweeney enquired rather lamely.

'Yes, students, Sergeant. Sir Arthur ran his Writers Guild business from home; he once proudly told me that he derived more pleasure from helping aspiring authors than any of his personal achievements in the literary field. Quite a statement when you consider a best seller career that must have spanned the best part of forty years.'

A uniformed police constable approached, 'Excuse me, Sir, forensics are on their way and we've cordoned off the murder scene at the rear of the house. Happened under a great chestnut tree in the main garden. Strange business, Sir. Looks like the victim's been shot with a bolt from a crossbow. Then his mouth's been stuffed with pages from one of his own books.'

'Okay Constable, good work. We'll let forensics do their job. First, let's interview everyone in the house. Where have you put them?' asked Parrot.

'The housekeeper, cook, and the gardener are in the kitchen. Sir Arthur's two sons and their wives are in the library, and there are twelve students from today's lecture in the seminar room.'

'Where's Lady Marjorie?'

'She's gone to London on a shopping trip with her daughter. They're due back any time now.'

Parrot grimaced, 'That's a conversation I'm not looking forward to having.'

Parrot and Sweeney headed for the kitchen where they found the gardener consoling the still distressed housekeeper. 'I believe you found Sir Arthur's body,' Parrot said.

The gardener slowly removed his arm from the housekeeper's slender shoulder and introduced himself as Martin Reynolds, then said, 'Yes that's right, this afternoon around four thirty. I'd been working in the greenhouse up till then. I fancied a coffee and a smoke. So I decided to take a break where I usually do at that time of the day, under the great chestnut on the main lawn.'

'When you discovered Sir Arthur's body, did you touch or remove anything in the immediate area?'

'No, Chief Inspector, I ran straight back to the main entrance. I saw Ms Silsbury and told her what had happened.'

'And you, Ms Silsbury, did you go to the main lawn to check out Mr Reynolds' story?'

'No. I called the police straight away. Why do you ask?'

'Well you seem to be very distraught, almost as though you had visited the murder scene yourself.'

'I am extremely upset, Chief Inspector. I've worked for Sir Arthur for twenty-three years and in all that time I've never known him to treat myself or any other person with anything but kindness and respect. He was a true gentleman, who cared about people and people's feelings.'

Parrot turned his attention back to the gardener, 'And how did you feel about Sir Arthur, Mr Reynolds?'

'Like Gwen said, he was a gentleman, always found time for a chat. We often passed the time of day when I was on my afternoon break, under the great chestnut. It was his favorite place on the estate. He would sit there with a malt whiskey and a Cuban cigar, and we would talk and put the world to rights.'

'Do you live at Headley Grange, Mr Reynolds?'

'Yes, I have a small cottage just by the main entrance.'

'And how long have you been in Sir Arthur's employ?'

'About four years; came up here after my wife passed away.'

'So you live alone?'

'No, I live with Simon, my youngest son. He helps me look after the estate.'

'And where is Simon at the moment?'

'It's his day off; he went to meet his girlfriend this morning. She lives in the village. He probably won't be back till late, if at all. He quite often stays over at her place.'

Parrot then turned to Ms Silsbury, 'Why was Sir Arthur in the garden and not in the lecture hall? I believe there are twelve students attending today's class?'

'Quite so Chief Inspector, but today's class was on the historical romantic novel, which would have been taken by Sir Arthur's eldest son Malcolm and his wife Sarah. As you probably know, Sir Arthur's forte is, I mean was, crime detection novels.'

'What about the other son and his wife, what do they teach?'

'Well, Lionel Messenger lectures on business studies and accountancy, and Paula, his wife, meets and greets and generally makes herself pleasant and agreeable, makes the tea and coffee, and passes the snacks around during the breaks.'

Parrot couldn't help but notice a slight edge of disdain in the housekeeper's voice as she described Paula Messenger's duties. 'Right,' Parrot said. 'I need you both to give your statements to Sergeant Sweeney and, more importantly, I have a question for you.' Looking directly at the cook, Parrot asked, 'Any chance of a cup of tea and a bite to eat? I'm famished.'

The ample sized, ruddy faced cook, whose name was Rose Fox chuckled heartily and said, 'How about a nice slice of apple pie with your tea?'

Whilst enjoying his pie, Parrot learned from Rose, that Gwen Silsbury had carried long and deep-seated feelings for Sir Arthur, and when twelve years ago, his first wife suddenly died, she saw herself as the new mistress of Headley Grange. Rose related the story with no malice. She explained that Gwen and herself had grown up together in the village and were friends and confidantes. However, there was malice when she then told of the scheming nature of Marjorie Hellman, who was Sir Arthur's publicist at the time and, according to Rose, was hell bent on becoming the new Lady Messenger. Gwen had little chance of competing with the elegantly groomed and worldly woman, who moved in different circles and name dropped with every sentence.

'So, Rose, the two boys are from Sir Arthur's first marriage. What about the daughter?'

'Oh her, little miss prim and proper. Airs and graces just like her mother. No, she's not Sir Arthur's.'

'Well, thanks, Rose. You've been a great help and thanks for the pie. Suppose I'd better head to the library.'

'Good luck with that,' Rose said with sarcasm and a smile.

Parrot entered the library, and introduced himself to Malcolm and Lionel Messenger and their wives Sarah and Paula. He then offered his sincere condolences, thanked the family for their patience, and apologized for the delay, all in one extended breath.

Malcolm Messenger stepped forward and shook hands with Parrot. 'Thank you, Chief Inspector. As you can imagine, we're all in a state of total shock. If you could keep the questions to a minimum for now, it really would be appreciated.'

'Yes, of course,' Parrot said sympathetically. 'I need each of you to go over your movements between one and four o'clock this afternoon. Sergeant Sweeney will take the details when I'm through here, which will not take long.

'Do any of you know of any reason why someone would want to harm your father and have you noticed any change in his behavior of late? Has he seemed pre-occupied or on edge? Anything out of character? It could be useful.'

Each of the four shook their heads, and then Lionel Messenger said, 'Dad did seem to have something on his mind a few weeks ago. I actually asked him if he was feeling okay. He just laughed and said he was fine, apart from being a bit tired. He laughed again, thanked me for my concern and, since then, he's been on top form as usual. It's hard to imagine anyone bearing him a grievance. He was an author and an educator for Christ sakes. Not a ruthless businessman with enemies.'

Parrot nodded in agreement. 'I met your father several times and you would find it difficult to meet a more likeable fellow. Which makes his murder all the more puzzling? So please, think hard in the next few days about anything that may shed some light on this case. It might be something that happened in the past that caught up with him. So any information, regardless of how seemingly unimportant, might just be the trig-ger to finding the murderer, and rest assured, I will find that person.'

Parrot caught up with his sergeant in the lecture room. 'I'm going to see what forensics can tell us; let me know if Lady Marjorie returns and better have a WPC on hand.'

'Ok, Sir, I'll see to it. Nothing much from the stu-dents. They seem to have been pretty much shut up in the lecture room for the day. That is, apart from their twelve o'clock break, when some of them did take a stroll round the gardens, but they were back by one o'clock, and we know Sir Arthur was still alive at the time.'

'First thing in the morning we need to set up a mobile incident room, Sergeant. Get on to division and organize enough men for a thorough sweep of the area. You know this was a very deliberate killing. Who shoots an elderly, respected man with a crossbow, then stuffs the old boy's mouth with pages from his own book? This smacks of revenge.'

Sweeney looked pensive. 'Have you read any of his novels, Sir?'

'No, I haven't, Sergeant, but there is one I am very anxious to read. Very anxious indeed.'

Darkness was closing in as Parrot reached the crime scene, where he was greeted by the head of Forensics, Dr. Harry Starkey, 'Hello George, what a turn up, I can't believe it. Arthur Messenger of all people. I only had dinner with him a couple of weeks ago.'

'How did he seem to you?'

'He seemed absolutely fine. He told me that he was working hard on his autobiography, which he was close to finishing.'

'What book do these pages come from?'

'From The Dove Dynasty, one of his most famous novels. Put him back on the literary map, so to speak.'

'Have you read it, Harry?'

'No, I see enough murder every day without spending my leisure time reading about it.'

'Same here. You know, it always seemed strange to me that a quiet, unassuming chap like Sir Arthur should be able to write so knowledgably about the bloodthirsty deeds of the underworld.'

'It crossed my mind too, George. In fact, I asked him that very question and he told me that he grew up watching American crime and suspense movies; he was totally hooked on the film noir genre by his early teens.'

'There must be a connection with this book, Harry. I guess I'm going to have to read the bloody thing.'

'Cheer up, George. You may actually enjoy the bloody thing.'

Parrot began to walk back to the castle, and with a backward wave to his long time friend and colleague, said, 'Goodnight, Harry. Let me have a full report in the morning.'

Reaching the Grange, Parrot caught up with Gwen Silsbury in the kitchen.

'Could you find one of Sir Arthur's books for me, please?'

'Certainly, Chief Inspector, which one do you require?'

'It's called The Dove Dynasty; I'm told it was his most successful novel.'

'Indeed it was. A huge best seller and of course when the Americans bought the film rights and made it into a smash hit at the box office, sales soared again.'

'I'm not much of a reader, but I can't recall a major film by that title.'

'That's understandable; the film company adapted the book for the US audience. They re-named it the Di Angelo Dynasty; I see by your reaction that you recognize the title.'

'Yes I do. Look, Ms Silsbury, you seem to know more about this place and the people living here than anybody. I really would appreciate your input, it's too late this evening, but would you be available for my sergeant tomorrow morning around ten thirty?'

'Yes of course, Chief Inspector. Now let me get that book for you.'

'Oh, just one more thing, how do you get on with Lady Marjorie?' The housekeeper smiled wryly. 'I don't,' she said. 'The truth of the matter is, if it was down to her, I would be long gone. We've never got on, but Sir Arthur always managed to smooth the tension between us, but I expect to get my marching orders any day now.'

'Well, perhaps it won't come to that,' Parrot said sympathetically. 'And even if it does, I'm sure you won't have any problem finding another position.'

'This has been my home for a long time, Chief Inspector, and I'm not sure I want another position. But there again, I'm not sure I want to stay on here anyway. I've saved some money, and Rose and I have talked about opening a little tea shop in the village. So we'll see what happens.'

'Well, good luck, whatever you decide,' Parrot said with genuine sincerity; he'd taken quite a liking to Gwen Silsbury and Rose Fox and had almost ruled them out as suspects.

Parrot's train of thought was broken by the arrival of Dan Sweeney. 'Lady Marjorie and her daughter have just returned. She got very agitated and insisted on knowing what was happening. Wouldn't take no for an answer, so I had to tell her. She and her daughter are in the main lounge with a WPC.'

'How did she take the news sergeant?'

'Quite well really, stiff upper lip I suppose. Asked me who was in charge? When I told her, she said that she had met you and demanded to see you immediately. I told her that you were interviewing the staff, but it didn't make any difference. I was instructed to find you and bring you to the lounge. She really is a very difficult woman, Sir, even allowing for the circumstances.'

'She is indeed, Sergeant, but I do need to see her, so come on; let's do as she asks.'

Parrot and Sweeney entered the lounge and Parrot said how sorry he was to meet her Ladyship again under these most tragic of circumstances. She studied him carefully as he spoke. 'The chief constable's banquet at the Guild Hall,' she said.

Parrot looked slightly bemused. 'I'm sorry, Lady Marjorie.'

'November, two years ago, the last time we met, Chief Inspector. You were there with your wife, Audrey.'

'My word, Lady Marjorie, what a memory you have.'

'Never forget a face or a name, Mr Parrot. Comes from being a bookworm. By the way, this is my daughter Vivien, and as you can imagine we are quite traumatized by these events.'

'I entirely understand. There's no need to trouble either of you further this evening. We'll save our questions for tomorrow morning.'

Parrot and Sweeney walked to the car and the sergeant said, 'If that's being traumatized, I'd love to see how she reacts to good news.'

Parrot smiled. 'She would react in exactly the same manner. Show no emotion, the motto of the nobility.'

'Excuse me, Sir, but she's not exactly royalty. I mean marrying a baronet hardly gets you any nearer to the throne.'

'You are missing the point, Sergeant. Being born noble requires acceptance and understanding of the fact but requires little or no change in personality, but some people who attain a higher social standing believe they should act and behave in away befitting their new status, and I guarantee that the then Marjorie Hellman read everything she could lay her hands on about the nobility and etiquette.'

Audrey Parrot greeted her husband with a kiss and a glass of beer. 'You look tired, George, rough day?'

'Yeah, you could say that, been up at the castle all night. Sir Arthur Messenger's been murdered.'

'Oh no. Who would want to kill a lovely man like that?'

'That's what I've been saying and hearing all evening, but someone out there had a reason, and I think I might just find the answer in this book.' He handed the book to her.

'*The Dove Dynasty*,' Audrey said, studying the cover. 'A great read, one of his best. Let me get your dinner, and I'll run you through it.'

Later, as Parrot tucked into his shepherd's pie, Audrey began to tell her husband the story of *The Dove Dynasty*.

'It's an epic crime book chronicling the Dove family over two generations,' she began. 'Apparently, it's based on a real-life East End crime gang that started up just after the Second World War, and it follows the family's fortunes through to the early eighties. It struck me as a bit like the cockney Godfather.'

'Audrey, do you remember if anyone was murdered by a shaft from a crossbow, and then had their mouth stuffed with pages from a book?'

'Was that how Sir Arthur was killed? Oh how dreadful, but I don't remember anything as macabre as that; there were plenty of shootings and vicious fights and some nasty stabbings, the sort of thing you'd expect but, no,' Audrey paused in mid sentence. 'Wait a minute, yes, there was a crossbow shooting. One of the Dove boys was ambushed by a rival gang and beaten to death and the head of the Dove family and his eldest son discovered that he had been betrayed by one of their brother's closest friends, who had tipped off this other gang as to where he would be alone at a certain time. I seem to remember the boy was leaving his girlfriend's apartment when he was attacked. Anyway, they took the informer to a warehouse they owned. Forced a confession out of him, and then tied him to a post, and Philip Dove, the eldest son, shot him through the chest with a metal shaft. I'm sure they didn't stuff his mouth with anything though.'

'Audrey, you've been a great help as usual. I suppose I should read the thing; it's a bit late this evening, though. I'll give it a go tomorrow. How many of his books have you read?'

'Every one he ever wrote. Always been a great fan of his.'

'What did you think of *The Dove Dynasty*?'

'I read it two or three times, full of pace and suspense and underworld intrigue, a bit gruesome at times but a great read.'

'Do you think it was his best?'

'It certainly was different from his normal genre. I mean a sweeping history of post-war crime in London, intermingled with the everyday family life of the members of a major crime syndicate, was a major break from his usual Police thriller mysteries. Though I do remember Sir Arthur telling me that he grew up in a rough part of East London, so maybe his background gave him some good first-hand material for the novel.'

'Could be, you know he once told me that, although he didn't appreciate it at the time, but growing up in a poor environment had given him a perspective and a strong work ethic in his later life. That was Sir Arthur, alright, amazingly successful, yet full of humility and good grace. I can't help feeling that there is a dark secret at the back of his murder, and I'm convinced this book holds the key.'

Parrot and Sweeney arrived at the castle early the following morning. A mobile incident room had already been set up and a major search of the grounds and the castle had begun at first light, without any major discoveries.

'Well, Sir, what's the plan of attack?' an eager Sweeney asked.

'Sergeant, I want you to talk to Rose Fox and then Gwen Silsbury. They're a mine of knowledge about the Messenger family. Concentrate on the time before and after the publication of *The Dove Dynasty*. Also see what you can find out about Lady Marjorie. I'm going to talk to her but I don't expect to get much information, unless I use a tire lever to prise it out of her.'

'Will you question the two sons and their wives, Sir?'

'Yes, but later. I also want another crack at Martin Reynolds, and I need to talk to his son. There's something that's bugging me about them. Let's meet up at lunchtime and compare notes. There's a nice pub just down the road and it's your turn to buy me a pie and a pint.'

Parrot smiled knowingly at his sergeant, who in turn said, 'Of course, Sir, looking forward to it already.'

'Oh, and before you head off to the kitchen for your breakfast, get on to division. I want thorough background checks on everyone at the castle and also on those twelve students who were here yesterday.'

'I'll get on it straight away. Will you be having breakfast with the family, Sir?'

'Certainly not. Luckily I have a caring wife who delights in sending me off each morning with a good, old-fashioned full English breakfast inside of me, and who am I to spoil her little pleasures?' said Parrot, chuckling again at his very own particular brand of humor.

So later, with the two policemen cozily ensconced in a quiet corner of the Barley Mow public house, Parrot said, 'Okay, sergeant, what have you got for me besides this delicious homemade chicken pie?'

'Well, you were bang on about Rose and Gwen, Sir. Nothing much gets past those two, and they were both more than happy to dish the dirt. Especially Rose, who seems to have a special dislike for Lady Marjorie and her daughter. Apparently, neither of them get on with Sir Arthur's sons or their wives. Feelings that are reciprocated with the exception of Paula, who does make an effort to be pleasant. Then again, as Rose told me, Paula is pleasant to everyone.'

'Are there any grandchildren?' asked Parrot.

'Yes, Sir, Malcolm and Sarah have two boys, James and Martin. They're sixteen and thirteen and both go to boarding school. Lionel and Paula have a ten-year-old girl named Gemma, who is staying with Paula's parents for a couple of weeks. Gwen told me that Sir Arthur was very much against the two boys going to boarding school. He used to say that Grammar school was good enough for him and that he hadn't done too badly, and a boy's place is with his family, not at some posh school where they can learn to be snotty adolescents. She also told me that Sir Arthur thought that the sun shone out of those two boys you-know-whats, and he was heartbroken when they left the castle to go to boarding school.'

Parrot took a large swig of beer to wash down his lunch, and then asked, 'Did Rose or Gwen say anything about Sir Arthur's relationship with Lady Marjorie?'

'Yes, they certainly did, Sir, especially Rose. She reckons Sir Arthur knew he had made a terrible mistake not long after the wedding, but he was a man of principle and decided to try to make the marriage work. Rose also said that Sir Arthur was so miserable with his new wife that his writing suffered for years, until he wrote *The Dove Dynasty*.'

'Now that is interesting,' Parrot said thoughtfully.

'What about the Writers Guild business? Was that Sir Arthur's idea?'

'Yes, that was his brainchild. Not very successful at first by all accounts. Lady Marjorie took it over and turned it into a going concern. Sir Arthur did insist that his two sons were on the board and, when they began to cater for day students, at very fancy prices, he brought Malcolm in to lecture on historical romance. As the company expanded, he found a place for Lionel to teach business studies. Not that he was particularly successful in that field according to Gwen.'

'Has Malcolm Messenger written any historical romance?'

'Yes indeed, Sir, quite successfully. Lady Marjorie is his publisher.'

'Seems an odd subject for a fellow.'

'Suppose it is. He writes under the name of Melissa Hopkirk. Ring any bells, Sir?'

'None whatsoever. Not my cup of tea.'

'Well, several of his novels have been dramatized for TV, and one was made into a film, which did very well in the States.'

'My word, you have been busy. Did your two confidantes say anything about our friend the gardener?'

'Gwen didn't have much to say, except that he was a nice bloke. Rose, on the other hand, was full of info. She reckons he's sweet on Gwen and they have been seeing each another for a couple of years. Apparently, he asked her to marry him months ago and she's still thinking it over.'

'What about his two boys?'

'Simon, his youngest is a quiet boy. He took his mum's death very hard. She was ill for some time before she passed. He would have been in his mid teens at that time. The eldest son, Duncan, lives in London. He works there for a large advertising company. He's a bit full of himself according to Rose, and here's the best part. When he was visiting his dad last year, he struck up a friendship with Vivien, and Rose reckons they've been seeing each other since.'

'Is that just conjecture or does she have proof?'

'She said Gwen caught them "at it", as she puts it, one afternoon in the library. She said the brazen hussy wasn't at all embarrassed, looked straight at Gwen and said, "Yes, can I help you?" without moving a muscle. Well, since then, Vivien has been spending a lot of time in London, and Rose thinks she has been meeting up with Duncan.'

'Well done, Sergeant, a good morning's work. More than I can say I'm afraid.'

'I take it that Lady Marjorie was not very helpful, Sir.'

'You take it right. A dreadful woman and that daughter of hers is not much better.'

'Did you ask her about *The Dove Dynasty?*'

'Of course. I asked her if Sir Arthur did a lot of research. How long it took him to write, and asked if he collaborated with anyone during the time he was writing his masterpiece. She became quite agitated. Said she couldn't remember and that she was very busy at that time running the Writers Guild. Then she asked me why I was asking her pointless questions, instead of tracking down her husband's murderer.'

'Does she know the details of the murder, Sir?'

'Yes, apparently Malcolm, or should I say *Sir* Malcolm, told her after we left last night. He told me when I questioned him this morning that he really didn't want to go into the manner of his father's murder, but Lady Marjorie, as is her way, insisted she be told. When he did tell her, she went as white as the proverbial sheet and almost fainted. Malcolm and Sarah helped her onto a settee and revived her with a glass of brandy.'

'So she is human, Sir.'

'Maybe, Sergeant, maybe. We'd better get back. I want to talk to Martin Reynolds and his youngest son.'

'What about Sir Arthur's will, Sir? Can we find out who benefits from his death before its made public?'

'Good thinking; call Harvey Brooks. He's a local solicitor at Brooks and Maybury. He looks after the Messenger family interests. Give him my regards and stress the importance of the will. See if you can meet him this afternoon. Shouldn't be a problem; he's a very accommodating fellow.'

Martin Reynolds was finishing his lunch when George Parrot entered the main greenhouse. 'Afternoon, Chief Inspector, care for a cup of coffee?'

'No thanks, Mr Reynolds, just need to ask you a few more questions,' Parrot said. 'The grounds of this place are huge. How do you manage to keep them in such immaculate condition with just help from your son?'

Reynolds laughed. 'If it were just the two of us, we wouldn't have time to eat or sleep. No I have a team of six and, sometimes, that's not enough.'

'Where were they yesterday? I didn't notice anyone in the gardens?'

'One was at college, two were working in the vegetable garden, and the other was in the small greenhouse. The local constable took their statements. I assumed he passed them on to you or your sergeant.'

'Are they local men?'

'Three are local men and the other one is a local girl.'

'Do they all work here full time?'

'Yes they all do, apart from young Jenny Penton. She does three days a week and spends the other two at the local college. She's taking a degree in horticulture.'

'Have you always been a gardener, Mr Reynolds?'

'Not always, Chief Inspector; when I left school, I joined the police force. I spent twelve years in uniform, five of them as a sergeant.'

'What made you join?'

'My father was a detective inspector. I grew up listening to his stories about crime in London. He made it sound very exciting somehow.'

'And what made you leave?'

'That's a good question. For the most part, I'd always loved the job. I'd been married for a few years, had a three-year-old and one on the way, and I began to resent the time I was spending away from them. But more than that, the area had become very dangerous. There was a huge increase in the drug trade. Violent crimes like muggings and stabbings became an everyday occurrence. The job suddenly became very dangerous and depressing, and I suddenly felt that I wasn't making a difference. My wife was worried sick every time I was on night duty. A couple of colleagues got badly beaten by a local gang. Two of the gang members were thirteen years old and one was a girl. Well, that was the last straw for June, my wife. It was ultimatum time. Either I got out or she was taking the boy and going to live with her parents. Well, she was six months pregnant, left me no choice. So I resigned and we moved to a quiet village in the country. I managed to get an assistant gardener's job at the local manor house.'

'Did you have any experience?'

'Only what I'd learnt from my dad at his allotment when I was a kid, He was a great one for his vegetables. Every Sunday he would present my mum with a sack of homegrown produce from one hand and a bunch of freshly cut flowers from the other. Then, when June and I bought our first house, we would spend every bit of spare time in the garden; it became a labor of love for both of us, and I was totally hooked. So I took a three-year correspondence course and got myself a decent diploma.'

'Does Simon share your passion?'

'Very much so. He's a quick learner. Gets it from his mum.'

'What about Duncan, Mr Reynolds? He works in advertising I believe?'

'That's right; bit of a high flier, my Duncan. He's doing very well. Wants to get to the top as quick as he can.'

'I'm told he's been seeing Vivien Hellman. How do you feel about that?'

'Do you have children Mr Parrot?'

'Yes, I have two daughters, why do you ask?'

'Are they married?'

'Yes they both are. Very happily as a matter of fact and, again, why do you ask?'

'Did you and your wife always approve of their husbands or previous boyfriends?'

'No, in all honesty I can't say that we did.'

'Well, in answer to your original question, no, I'm not jumping for joy that he's seeing her, but he will make his own choice and, as long as he's happy, then rather like yourself and your wife, I'll be happy as well.

'Parrot smiled and said, 'Point taken. Does Lady Marjorie know about their liaison?'

'Oh yes, there's not much that escapes that woman.'

'Has she spoken to you about their relationship?'

'Not so much spoken, as made her views perfectly clear about the unsuitability of their friendship, as she referred to it. Asked me to talk to Duncan and warn him off. I told her that my son's personal life was his own and I didn't think my talking to him about his choice would do anything other than to strengthen his resolve to continue seeing the young lady.'

'Did you indeed? Well, good for you, Mr Reynolds, how did she respond?'

'She said that we all have duties as parents to show our children the errors of their ways Not to do so is an abdication of that duty. I didn't have time to reply. She had already turned her back and was heading back to the castle before she had finished her lecture.'

'What's your opinion of Vivien Hellman?'

'I've only spoken to her a few times. She's got her mother's controlling ways, but nothing a good bloke couldn't sort out. I try not to be swayed by third-party gossip, Chief Inspector, so I can't really give you an opinion; Duncan likes her, but whether it goes any further than a bit of fun, you would have to ask him. I'd personally say no, but I could be completely wrong.'

'Alright, Mr Reynolds, that's all for the time being. Now I need to ask Simon a few questions. Where is he working at the moment?'

'He's down by the lake. Shall I call him for you?' Reynolds said, suddenly producing a walkie-talkie from his dungarees.

'No, don't bother. Just point me in the right direction, I'll find him,' Parrot said.

Strolling to the lake area, Parrot couldn't help but feel that the father would have made contact with the son before he arrived at his destination but that would only be natural, he surmised.

'Hello Simon, your dad told me you were down here. I'm Chief Inspector Parrot, and I'm investigating the murder of Sir Arthur Messenger. So I need to ask you some questions,' Parrot said, in an exaggerated, serious voice.

'Right,' the boy said quietly. 'What do you want to know?'

'Where were you yesterday? Your dad said you were with your girlfriend, is that correct?'

'Yes, from just after one o'clock, until eight o'clock this morning.'

'That's very precise, Simon, how did you spend yesterday morning?'

'I was up early, about half past six, and then I came down here to finish replanting on the other side of the lake.'

'That's very conscientious of you on your day off.'

'Ran out of daylight the night before, and I didn't have anything else to do. My girlfriend was at college taking a morning class that finishes at one o'clock. We met at the Barley Mow just after then for a drink.'

'Your girlfriend wouldn't happen to be Jenny Penton?'

'Yes, that's right; we've been going out for a few months.'

'Did you have much contact with Sir Arthur?'

'Not really. I saw him around the estate occasionally.'

'Did he speak to you?'

'Sometimes, just to say good morning or he'd ask me how I was getting on.'

'Did you see or talk to him yesterday morning?'

'I saw him; he was walking across the main lawn.'

'What time was this and was he alone?'

'It must have been around nine thirty, and he was with Vivien.'

'Could you hear what they were talking about?'

'No, they were too far away, but she did raise her voice and started to wave her arms about.'

'How do you get on with Vivien?'

'I don't really know her; we've hardly ever spoken.'

'Does your brother talk about her?'

'Not really. He says she's good fun, that's all.'

'So you don't think it's that serious between them?'

'From what little Duncan says, I reckon it's more serious on her part.'

'Is that so,' Parrot said. 'Okay, Simon, that's all for now.'

Dan Sweeney greeted him on his arrival at the incident room. 'Hello, Sir, just got back from talking to Mr Brooks, and you were right, he was very accommodating.'

'Judging from the beam on your face that I spotted from fifty yards away, Sergeant, I'd say you have some news for me.'

'I have, Sir. Wait till you hear the details of Sir Arthur's will.'

'Well, come on. I'm all ears, let's be having it.'

'Right, Headley Grange is left to his two sons on condition that they continue the Writers Guild business. They also each receive ten million pounds. The three grandchildren each get five million pounds, which is in trust until they are twenty-five. Now comes the interesting part, Sir. Lady Marjorie receives One million pounds, the London apartment, and an allowance of one hundred thousand pounds a year until her death. That is provided she resigns her directorship of the Writers Guild and plays no further part in its operation.'

'Her Ladyship will be incandescent when she hears this, Sergeant.'

'Wait till you hear the last part of his bequests, Sir.'

'Go on, I can hardly contain myself.'

'Rose Fox is left seventy five thousand pounds and an annuity of fifteen thousand until death and Gwen Silsbury receives half a million pounds and fifty thousand a year until death.'

'Lot of money for servants, Sweeney. Very generous indeed.'

'That's nothing; Sir Arthur has left five million pounds to Martin Reynolds and a million apiece to his two sons.'

'Good grief, Sergeant, what the hell's going on? Why on earth would he leave such an enormous amount of money to his gardener? Look, let's keep a lid on this. The reading of the will won't be until after the funeral. So that gives us at least a week to find the killer or killers. Any other surprises?'

'Not really, a few small bequests to friends and there are some generous charitable donations, and, before I forget, Sir, Dr. Starkey called. Says he got some interesting news.'

'How much more interesting can this case get, Sweeney? Ok, I'll call him straight away. In the meantime, I want you to question the two sons and their wives. See if you can find out if there was anything out of the ordinary happening around the time Sir Arthur was writing *The Dove Dynasty*. After I've spoken to Dr. Starkey, I need to talk to Vivien Hellman. Simon Reynolds saw her in the garden with Sir Arthur yesterday morning and she appeared to be very agitated about something and, after I'm finished with her. It's onto the main course with her mother.'

Parrot rang the doctor and, when Dr. Starkey came on the line, Parrot said, 'I believe you have something of interest for me, Harry?'

'Yes, George, nothing unusual about the murder; he was killed by a shaft fired from a crossbow from about ten feet, but, when I examined him further, I discovered that he was dying of advanced pancreatic cancer. He would have had three to four months at best. I called his doctor who confirmed the illness. Diagnosed six months ago. He said Sir Arthur refused to see a specialist, said his time was up and he was going to enjoy what remained of his life and that he wasn't interested in any new revolutionary treatment. Let them find another lab rat to try out their experiments. Sounds like him doesn't it?'

'Sure does. Let Sweeney have the name and address of the doctor, please, Harry. We'll need him to make a statement.'

Parrot found Vivien Hellman sprawled out on a sofa in the main lounge. She was laughing loudly, evidently at something the person on the other end of the line had said. Parrot coughed and said, 'Excuse me, Miss Hellman; I need an urgent word with you.'

'Can't it wait? I'm rather tied up at the moment,' she said irritably.

'I suggest you hang up now or I will question you at the local police station, which I can assure you has far less comfortable surroundings.'

She looked at Parrot with a brief air of defiance and then said, 'Sorry darling, have to go, PC Plods here, catch you later.'

Parrot ignored the sleight and said, 'Its Chief Inspector Plod, actually, now Miss Hellman, just a few questions. First, can you tell me why you were arguing with your stepfather in the garden yesterday morning around nine thirty?'

She fixed him with narrowed, spiteful eyes. 'It was a private matter, with no bearing whatsoever on your investigation.'

Parrot could hear Lady Marjorie's influence in her daughter's sharp delivery, and he steeled himself. 'I will be the judge of that. Now, at the risk of repeating my-self. If I don't receive satisfactory answers, you will be taken, forcibly if necessary, to the station. This is a mur-der investigation and I urge you most ardently not to treat what I'm saying as an idle threat.'

'If you must know, we were talking about my allow-ance. I asked him for an increase and he refused.'

'Did you discuss Duncan Reynolds with Sir Arthur?'

'As a matter of fact I did.'

'What was the exact nature of the discussion?'

'I asked him to have a word with Mummy; you see she doesn't approve of my seeing the gardener's son.'

'What was Sir Arthur's response?'

'He said that he made it a point of not interfering in personal matters, said that he had not done so with his own children and wasn't about to start with me.'

'So I dare say you were upset that he denied both your requests?'

'Not really, I just wanted him to get my mother off my back; she's driving me round the bend. She's con-stantly on my case about how unsuitable Duncan is and reminding me of our position.'

'And the allowance refusal?'

'I knew he would refuse, but I thought if I asked him for an increase first, then he was less likely to turn me down over the Duncan and mother thing, I was wrong.'

'Did you talk about anything else?'

'No, he turned me down. I think I called him a mean old sod and went directly back to the castle.'

'What time did you and Lady Marjorie leave for your day trip?'

'We caught the ten-forty train to London and arrived at eleven thirty.'

'Did you spend the whole day together?'

'Good grief no. I'd arranged to meet Duncan for lunch. Then we went back to his apartment for the afternoon. In actual fact, lunch was a very quick drink. I haven't seen him for ten days, if you catch my drift.'

'Yes, quite,' Parrot said somewhat uncomfortably. 'So when did you meet up with Lady Marjorie?

'On the train. Duncan asked me to stay over but I couldn't face the prospect of another scene with her.'

'Did Lady Marjorie say how she spent the day?'

'She said that she'd met some friends for lunch. Spent some time shopping in Harrods, and then went back to the apartment for a couple of hours.'

Parrot thanked her for being cooperative, and then set off to find Lady Marjorie. He was under no illusion that the strong-arm tactics employed on the daughter, would be of any use to force the compliance of the mother. He found her in the library and, in his best acquiescent voice said, 'Excuse me, Lady Marjorie, I wonder if you feel up to answering a few questions,' whilst inside not caring a tinkers fart whether she was really up to it or not.

'Oh, yes, I suppose so, Chief Inspector, but not for too long, I'm still feeling rather weak, you understand.'

'Of course. Can you tell me how you spent the day in London yesterday?'

'I met some friends for a few drinks around half past twelve. Then three of us had lunch at the Dorchester, after which I did some shopping in Harrods. Then I went back to my apartment at half past four. I relaxed for a couple of hours then got a taxi to the station.'

'Forgive me, Lady Marjorie, after lunch, how did you spend the rest of the afternoon?'

'Is that really at all relevant, Chief Inspector?'

'Filling in the dots, Lady Marjorie, nothing sinister I assure you.'

'Well, as a matter of fact, I did spend the afternoon with Leslie Burkett, a very old and dear friend.'

'Sorry to be pedantic, your Ladyship, would that be Mr or Mrs Leslie Burkett?'

'That would be Mr Burkett, Chief Inspector,' she said stone-faced.

'May I now ask you about your daughter and Duncan Reynolds? I believe you disapprove of their friendship.'

'Quite so. I have nothing personal against the boy you understand. It's just that he's not right for Vivien.'

'She appears to be very fond of him.'

'Duncan Reynolds has a winning way about him, and Vivien is still quite young and very impressionable. I think their relationship will blow itself out in due course.'

'Lady Marjorie, I hope you will forgive me, but I need to ask you some personal questions about your marriage to Sir Arthur.'

'If you really must,' she said, and then sensing Parrot's hesitation added, 'Well, come on, man, what do you wish to know?'

'I believe you married Sir Arthur twelve years ago and, before that, you were his publisher, is that correct?'

'Yes, I worked for the company that published Sir Arthur's works. I was given the account about eighteen years ago. We became close friends, and when his first wife died, he was devastated and turned to me for comfort.'

'What about Vivien's father?'

'He was, as they say, a mistake; we divorced when Vivien was very young.'

'Does she see him?'

'No, he died ten years ago.'

'Would you say that you and Sir Arthur had a happy marriage?'

'Well, Chief Inspector, I suppose it depends on how you define *happy*. We had a good relationship. Was he the love of my life? No. Was I the love of his? Again no. He was nearly twenty years older than me and we had different interests, different friends and, to be frank, different lives but we got on and I am genuinely upset by his death.'

'Thank you, Lady Marjorie, can you throw any light on his murder. Do you know of any connection between *The Dove Dynasty* and any potential suspects? I'm convinced there is a link somewhere.'

'I can't help you, Chief Inspector. I know of no connection.'

'Can you tell me about The Writers Guild?'

'There's not much to tell. Arthur was always interested in helping young writers, so he started the Guild about fifteen years ago, but as good as his philanthropic intentions were, he was no businessman. He neglected his own writing whilst trying to help others with theirs, and over time both suffered.

'He asked for my help and I managed to turn the business around by outsourcing most of the donkeywork.

He wouldn't give it up completely; he enjoyed giving advice and encouragement.'

'How does the Guild function on a practical level?'

'Students are set assignments. Easy one pagers at first, covering various day-to-day topics. Then they are given increasingly more difficult storylines. Their progress is closely monitored, and their work is read and graded by published authors of varied genres, whom we retain.'

Parrot thanked Lady Marjorie for her patience and frankness and began to leave. He suddenly turned and said, 'Oh, by the way, how's Sir Arthur's health been during the last year?'

'He seemed fine to me, he wasn't one to complain.'

He thanked her again and made his way to the incident room where he caught up with Dan Sweeney.

'Hello, Sir, how did it go with the duchess and her daughter?' he said with more than a trace of sarcasm.

'Very whimsical, Sergeant; as a matter of fact, quite the reverse of what I expected. Makes me more suspicious than ever about the pair of them.'

'Care to explain that, Sir?'

'Lady Marjorie, whilst appearing both frank and yet at the same time slightly peeved, is a consummate exponent in the art of the half truth. A dubious talent that her daughter also has in abundance. Add their undoubted cunning and ruthless natures, and you get a couple of very plausible suspects. Though I doubt either actually committed the murder. We need to check, and when I say *we*, Sergeant, I of course mean *you* need to check their alibis for yesterday in London. Lady Marjorie spent the latter part of the afternoon with a

Leslie Burkett at her apartment. Get her to give you his details and run a check on her first husband. She said he died ten years ago and, when you've done that, get Duncan Reynolds' address. We need, and when I say *we*, Sergeant, I of course mean *I* need to take a trip to question him.'

'Well, I'm pleased to say, Sir, that I can save you a journey. I spoke to Duncan Reynolds earlier, and you will be pleased to know that he will be here at ten-thirty tomorrow morning,' Sweeney said with as straight a face as he could muster.

'Did you manage to get anything new from Malcolm and Lionel Messenger?'

'Not a great deal, Sir. They told me that their father was stricken with grief when their mother died and his work suffered as a result. They begrudgingly gave Lady Marjorie some credit for his recovery. Though they plainly have little fondness for her or her daughter.'

'I'm not sure who exactly has much fondness for the pair of them; I'm not even sure they like each other,' Parrot remarked with a wry grin, then added, 'Well I'm off home now, and being that most generous of people, I shall be taking Mrs Parrot out for a slap up meal this evening. See you here tomorrow at nine o'clock sharp, when I shall eagerly await the arrival of Duncan Reynolds.'

During dinner that evening, Audrey Parrot mentioned to her husband, 'I don't know if it's important, George, but I seem to remember reading many years ago, in one of those society columns, that Marjorie's first husband was a bit of a bad lot; I think he was sent to prison.'

'Can you remember what for? Your dessert may depend on it.'

'In that case, I'll have to forego dessert; though I'm sure I read it was around the time she and Sir Arthur were getting married. I recall thinking at the time what nasty mind sets out to cause someone pain and deliberately spoil their wedding day.'

'Nasty minds like that prevail because they are nourished by people who need their daily intake of gossip and vitriol; apparently those two ingredients are necessary to sell newspapers.'

'My word, George, that's very profound.'

'Yes, you're right, far too heavy, let's change the subject. Why do you think Sir Arthur left his gardener five million pounds in his will?'

'Well, off the top of my head, he could be his illegitimate son. Or a legitimate son of his first wife that he knew nothing about until recently. Or maybe he gave up baby Martin for adoption when he was young and poor.'

'Your dessert has just been reinstated. I sometimes think you could do my job quite easily, but then you would have to endure my limited culinary skills. Not much to look forward to after a long day chasing villains.'

'The pleasure of your company would be food enough for me, George.'

'My dear, your honesty and perception has earned you a coffee and a liqueur of your choice.'

Audrey raised her hands to her neck and, in her best deep-southern American accent said, 'Why, George Parrot, I do declare, you spoil me something awful.'

'Find me this killer, Miss Audrey, and my generosity will know no bounds,' replied Parrot, in a dialect more akin to the southwest of England than South Carolina.

'I don't remember Rhett Butler having a West country accent, George, but if they ever consider a sequel set in Devon, you'll be perfect for the part, but seriously, are you anywhere near solving Sir Arthur's murder?'

'I'm getting close and everyone of interest as they say will be at the castle tomorrow. So I forecast an eventful day.'

Early the following morning, Parrot rang Dan Sweeney and arranged to meet up at the village café.

'Mrs Pol…I mean Parrot not cooking you a breakfast today, Sir?'

'That would be correct, Sergeant. Mrs Parrot is having a well-deserved lay in after providing invaluable assistance in this case. She tells me that Marjorie Messenger's first husband was a bad lot and thinks he may have gone to prison. She also came up with three plausible reasons why Martin Reynolds should be left five million quid.'

'Well she's dead right about the husband Sir. A nasty piece of work by the name of Donald Sangster. Three convictions for GBH and one for attempted murder for which he was sentenced to fifteen years.'

'So he died in prison?'

'He didn't die at all, Sir. He was released six months ago and, according to his parole officer, he is living in

West London in an apartment owned by none other than Lady Marjorie Messenger. Do you want him picked up, Sir?'

'Yes, get onto Scotland Yard. I want him brought to the castle this afternoon.'

'Are you going to question Lady Marjorie this morning?'

'Oh yes sergeant. Let's give her some nice long rope. You know I never thought I'd hear myself saying this, but I'm looking forward to talking to her Ladyship, very much indeed. I'll see you in the café in twenty minutes, Sergeant and if you get there before me, mine's a full English breakfast.'

During breakfast, Parrot told his sergeant that he wanted him to talk to Simon Reynolds as soon as they arrived at the castle. 'Use your tact and see if you can get some background info on the family around the time of Mrs Reynolds illness and death. Meanwhile, I think it's about time I asked Martin Reynolds about his inheritance. Let's meet up after that, to question Duncan Reynolds on his arrival. Then we can tackle her Ladyship. So a busy morning ahead, Sergeant, let's make some headway. I don't want the chief constable on my back. You know what he's like with unsolved high-profile cases.'

'Yes, Sir, is it my turn to pay for breakfast?'

'Why not, Sergeant. It's a working breakfast. Put in an expense chit and I'll sign it.'

Parrot found Martin Reynolds sharing a flask of coffee with Gwen Silsbury in the small greenhouse.

'Sorry to interrupt, but I need to ask Mr Reynolds a few questions.'

The housekeeper looked a little flustered. 'I'd better get back,' she said. 'See you this evening, Martin. Good morning, Chief Inspector.'

The two men watched her head back to the castle, and then Parrot turned to the gardener. 'A fine woman, Mr Reynolds. You're a lucky man to have such a loyal friend.'

'More than just a friend, Mr Parrot, she agreed to marry me last night.'

'Well, many congratulations. I'm sure that you'll both be very happy.'

'You know, when my wife died I was devastated, I never dreamt that I would find such happiness again. Then I met Gwen and she has totally rebuilt my life.'

'Will you stay on at the castle?'

'Unlikely, Gwen seems sure that Lady Marjorie will sack her after the funeral. So I guess we will look for a vacancy where we can work together.'

'Are you expecting a bequest in Sir Arthur's will?'

'Well, he did tell me that I was a beneficiary, but I don't suppose I will be retiring on the proceeds.'

'What if I told you, that he has left you half a million pounds?'

'I'd say that was incredibly generous.'

'I think it's time for the pair of us to stop shadow boxing, Mr Reynolds. I need to know exactly why Sir Arthur thought to leave you such a large sum and please the truth. I don't want to take you to the station, but I will if necessary and I will bring Gwen down there as well. You see, she has also been left a considerable amount of money, and with the two of you being so close, there are grounds to link the pair of you to the murder.'

'Mr Parrot, I swear that Gwen and I had nothing to do with his murder. We both loved the old boy. We could never harm him.'

'I'm inclined to believe you, but I need to know why he left you so much money. It has something to do with *The Dove Dynasty*, doesn't it?'

The resignation on the gardener's face was all too evident that Parrot's shot in the dark had found its mark.

'Come on, Martin. If you loved Sir Arthur, help me find his killer.'

'Ok, I'll tell you what happened. I mentioned that my dad was a policeman and I grew up hearing all about the underworld and crime in South London. Well, my wife June was always on at me to write a book about The Davies Boys. They were a larger than life crime family with a finger in every pie imaginable. Well, I'd never written anything before, so I decided to enroll in The Writers Guild for some guidance. They started me off with small assignments, and I received encouragement and praise for my efforts and, after about six months, I was asked to write a story of about a hundred pages. This was an ideal opportunity to commit The *Davies Boys*, to paper. I worked every night after work for about a month, sometimes till three or four o clock in the morning. I can't tell you the number of rewrites I made, but finally I managed to set down all my father's wonderful renderings, that had me so entranced as a kid. I sent the story to the Guild then waited. I didn't hear anything for about a month. Then I received my story back with untold corrections and a letter stating that whilst my story showed some promise it was written in an amateurish fashion and the market for crime novels was at saturation point. They suggested I try another genre but my one story was *The Davies Boys*, I was under no illusion about my literary talents, Mr Parrot. They say everyone has a book inside them, well that was mine, so I decided to call it a day. June did keep on at me to send the story to a publisher, but I was feeling so discouraged that I lost heart. I'd worked so hard on the story, and to be shot down in flames by so-called experts left me feeling totally deflated.

'Anyway, we got on with our life and forgot all about the book until about three years later when June told me that she had just finished reading a best seller by Sir Arthur Messenger called, *The Dove Dynasty*, and that she thought it was a masked and padded version of *The Davies Boys*. So I read the book and, although it was four hundred pages long and contained much of his own material, it seemed to me that he had skillfully interwoven my story into the novel.'

'So did you confront Sir Arthur, given he was the founder of the Guild and you had your returned story?'

'That was my initial thought. So I went to a solicitor for advice. He told me that my case was at best tenuous and that Sir Arthur's reputation was such that any legal action, apart from being costly, was almost bound to fail.'

'Did you then approach Sir Arthur directly?'

'No, it wasn't long after that my wife was taken ill and all my energy was taken up looking after her; the next two years were the worst time of my life.'

'You must have been very bitter; the royalties from your story would have paid for the best care for your wife.'

'I'm not going to lie to you; watching my wife die slowly crippled me inside. If Sir Arthur had stood before me at that time, I would have gladly driven a knife into his black heart. Then everyday to watch my two boys see their mother slowly slip away. Well it was the darkest of times.'

'So did you come here for revenge?'

'Partly, but I'd heard so much about Sir Arthur's courage and generosity and, after watching him being interviewed on TV, it was hard to imagine him lowering himself to steal another person's thoughts. It seemed beneath him.'

'Did your two boys know about your story?'

'Yes, their mum got them involved when I began to write. It was all very exciting at the time.'

'Did they also know that Sir Arthur had usurped your work?'

'I told Duncan after June died, but I never mentioned anything to Simon. He's a sensitive lad and took his mum's death very hard.'

'So you couldn't say for sure that Duncan hasn't told his younger brother about your suspicions?'

'Not definitely, but I made it very clear to Duncan at the time that I didn't want Simon involved. He understood and promised me that he would keep it to himself.'

'So moving forward, how come Sir Arthur didn't recognize you as the *Davies Boys* author when you started work at the castle?'

'Because I used an alias to write the story. TD Armitage actually. Sounds so pretentious now. Anyway, we lived in an annex to the manor house at my last job, and the post would arrive at the main hall. I didn't want anyone there to know about my writing, so I used a local Post Office box number and an alias as camouflage. It all seemed to add to the excitement back then.'

'So how exactly did Sir Arthur learn your secret?'

'Well, it was about eighteen months ago. We were chatting as had become our routine, under the great chestnut tree. It was a beautiful early spring evening and, as usual, he was enjoying single malt and a Cuban cigar. Both of which were definitely not his first of the day when, suddenly, he asked me if I had ever done anything to be ashamed of. It totally took me by surprise and, frankly, I stumbled around for an answer. He looked very sad and said that he had always tried to live an honorable life but that he was eaten up with guilt about a terrible injustice he'd committed.

'I knew at once he was referring to *The Dove Dynasty,* and he continued to tell me the whole story of his unremitting grief over the death of his first wife that led to his mental breakdown and how Lady Marjorie had rescued him from despair. Albeit at an ongoing price of total anguish. How she came to him with a story of a crime family written by a member of the Guild. He never laid the blame on his wife as he related the account, although I could hear that woman's voice badgering him constantly to use the material. Instead, he took full responsibility for his weakness. He went on to tell me that, after the novel was a best seller, he tried to make reparation but the contact address he had was

defunct and, short of advertising his guilt, he was power-
less to do anything. He said that the continued success
of the book and the numerous awards did nothing but
heighten his guilt to unbearable levels.'

'My God, Martin, what must have been going through
your mind?'

'Well, Mr Parrot, I had long since forgiven him.
You see the book he wrote was far removed from my
work. I had just been a catalyst and, besides, I had a
genuine affection for the man and to hear him pour
his heart out was gut wrenching. His suffering was absolutely genuine, and I had this perfect opportunity to
take his pain away. So I put an arm around his shoulder
and very quietly said, TD Armitage wants you to know
that he forgives you and bears you only good will. He
slowly looked up at me. His face was contorted in dis-
belief. I nodded as sincerely as I could manage, and
then went on to tell him the whole story, and I have
never seen a man sob uncontrollably for so long. It was
as though all his years of pent up guilt and self-loathing
were being violently expunged from his being. When
he finally regained a sense of composure, he told me
that he must make amends: "If you need anything," he
said, "just name it." I told him that my life was just fine.
My two boys were happy and doing well. I loved my job
and Gwen and I had grown quite close and every day I
looked forward to our afternoon chats. He smiled and
said that he thought that Gwen and I made an ideal
couple and that he wasn't going to wish us luck because
he was sure we didn't need it. He then said Duncan and
Simon were a credit to me but to tell Duncan to be careful about Vivien. I said that he could take care of himself

and that he was born clever. He then said, "That's as well as maybe, but she is her mother's daughter alright and then some." That was it really, he repeated if there was anything I needed, to just ask and I said that I would.'

Parrot looked sternly at the gardener. 'That's quite a story, Martin, and one that I'm inclined to believe. I understand you wanting to protect your boys but I wish you had told me sooner.'

'Yes, Mr Parrot, you're right, I should have. I can only offer fatherly concern as an excuse.'

'Does Gwen know about your story?'

'No, I've never mentioned anything to her.'

'Alright, Martin, that's all for now. I shouldn't really tell you this, but Sir Arthur's bequest to you is not five hundred thousand pounds at all.'

'That was a cheap shot then, Chief Inspector.'

'Not really. I needed to see your reaction. If I had told you the truth, that he has left you five million pounds, you might not have been so forthcoming.' With a wave of his hand, Parrot headed back to the castle where he caught up with Dan Sweeney.

'Get anything from young Simon?'

'Not really, Sir, he seems like a nice lad. I can't see him being mixed up in Sir Arthur's murder. Anyway, his girlfriend verifies his whereabouts. What about you, Sir, any luck with the gardener?'

'You could say that,' said Parrot, and then proceeded to tell his trusted sergeant what he had learned. 'Do you believe him, Sir?'

'Yes I do. Martin Reynolds had genuine affection for the old boy. You should have seen the look on his face when I told him that he'd been left five million quid, quite made my day.'

'Well, I don't want to spoil it so early, Sir, but we've had a call from the Yard, seems Donald Sangster has done a bunk.'

'Not to worry. I have a feeling he's quite nearby.'

'You think he's mixed up in this, Sir?'

'I'd stake a year's worth of Mrs Parrot's full English breakfasts sergeant; now let's see if Duncan Reynolds has arrived.'

Arriving at the incident room, the two policemen were greeted by a smartly dressed young man, drinking a cup of police coffee and smoking a large cigar. He introduced himself as Duncan Reynolds and asked how he could be of help. Parrot's first impression was that the descriptions he had received about the young man as being a bit full of himself appeared to be true. Although he seemed more confident than arrogant. Parrot fixed him with a steely look and said, 'Yes, Mr Reynolds, I think you can be of great help. I believe you spent the day of Sir Arthur's murder with Vivien Hellman in London at your apartment?'

'Yes that's right; we met for a quick drink, and then went back to my place.'

'Did you have any contact with anyone else during that time?'

'No, we spent the whole day alone.'

'Any phone calls or deliveries?'

'I got a call on my mobile around two-thirty from a colleague about a problem with a presentation I'm heading for a major client.'

'Why didn't this colleague call you on your landline?'

'Because I give my home phone number to very few people, Chief Inspector, and, anyway, Vivien and I didn't want to be disturbed, so we took the phone off the hook.'

'So in essence, Mr Reynolds, you and Ms Hellman are each other's alibis?'

'Yes, I suppose we are. Is that a problem?'

'Could be. Do you have underground parking at your apartment building?'

'Yes we have. I'm sorry I don't get the connection.'

'The connection is that you could have driven to the castle that morning. Probably wouldn't have taken you more than an hour if you had left early. Laid in wait for Sir Arthur, shot him, then drove back and slipped back into your apartment via the underground garage, where your accomplice and alibi was waiting for you.'

'That's totally untrue. What earthly reason did I have to kill him?'

'How about revenge for what he did to your father?'

'My father thought the world of Sir Arthur. Sure, years ago, there was some animosity, but that's history, and if I was so full of revenge why would I wait until now?'

'Did you tell Vivien about your father's story and what Sir Arthur had done?'

'No, I never mentioned anything. My father told me not to tell a soul, said it was all in the past and best forgotten. So I forgot about it as well.'

'Forgive me for asking, but are you and Vivien planning to get married?'

Reynolds burst out laughing, then said, 'Good Lord, no, we're just having a good time. Look she's fun to be with but this is strictly short term.'

'How do you get on with Lady Marjorie?'

'She's a pain Chief Inspector, always on Vivien's case about the family name. She's the archetypal "come into money" snob. I wouldn't mind, but she was once married to some thug who's in prison.'

'So you know about Donald Sangster?'

'Oh, is that his name? Only the little that Vivien's told me about him.'

'Did she tell you that he was released on parole six months ago?'

'No, she didn't, but I don't suppose she knows herself; they didn't exactly keep in touch.'

'Getting back to you and Vivien, do you think she's serious about your relationship?'

'She calls me her bit of rough and I tell her she's my bit of posh. No she's not serious about us. If she were, we wouldn't be together.'

'Alright, that's all for now. Are you driving back to London this evening?'

'No, I'm here for a few days, staying with my dad.'

'Ok, I'll need to speak to you again, so don't go wandering without letting me know.'

'I was planning to take Vivien down to the coast tomorrow.'

'I'd prefer both of you to stay local for the next few days. We will have more questions for Ms Hellman and yourself. In fact, we would like to interview you together.

Shall we say ten o'clock tomorrow morning?' With that, Parrot beckoned to his sergeant to accompany him to the castle.

'Is it Lady Marjorie time, Sir?'

'Yes, Sweeney, it is, and I want you to conduct the interview. Initially anyway. Being interviewed by a detective sergeant, with me in attendance is bound to ruffle her feathers. What's your opinion of Duncan Reynolds?'

'Well, like you said, Sir, he's a bit too sure of himself, but he's likeable and seems a decent bloke.'

'My thoughts entirely, although I'm not totally convinced by his manner. I'd say he has a much softer persona than he would care to admit.'

The two policemen found Lady Marjorie in the library. She asked them to sit down, to which Sweeney replied, 'Thanks, Lady Marjorie, we won't keep you too long. Just a few questions.' Parrot moved over to the window distancing himself from the proceedings, to the obvious annoyance of Lady Marjorie. Sweeney coughed to attract her attention, and then said, 'Yesterday, when Chief Inspector Parrot questioned you about Donald Sangster, your first husband, you replied that he was dead. Is there anything you wish to change about that comment?' She began to fidget nervously, obviously not being used to being challenged; her discomfort was all too evident. 'Well is there?' prompted the sergeant, which just heightened her agitated demeanor.

'When I said that he was dead, I was talking metaphorically; he has been dead to me for many years.'

'Are you aware that he was released from prison six months ago?'

'I have had absolutely no knowledge of him for fifteen years.'

'So you have had no contact with him since he was released?'

'None whatsoever.'

'Have you received any correspondence from him, either when he was in prison or since his release?'

She fixed Sweeney with a stern look of contempt and said, 'At the risk of continually repeating myself, no contact of any kind, by word of mouth, by letter, by e-mail, or by bloody carrier pigeon, is that clear enough for you?'

Sweeney had done his job and Parrot swiftly took over saying, 'Please don't upset yourself, Lady Marjorie, we both appreciate the trying circumstances you are under,' at the same time giving his sergeant an admonishing look of disapproval that her Ladyship was intended to see. 'It's just that difficult questions have to be asked if we are going to catch Sir Arthur's murderer.'

Put at her ease, she began to relax, 'Thank you Chief Inspector, I appreciate your consideration.'

Parrot smiled and softly said, 'If you don't mind me asking, you and your first husband seem an unlikely pairing. How did you happen to marry?'

'A very good question and one that I've asked myself on countless occasions. Well, when I first met Donald Sangster, I had no idea that he was mixed up with criminal elements. He was very clever to keep his connections quiet. I genuinely thought he was a legitimate businessman, which indeed he was, but I later found he was also mixed up in drug dealing, prostitution, and extortion. Donald was a smooth talker and had a way with the ladies, Mr Parrot. Something I also found out much later. I suppose at the time, he seemed exciting. He was very attentive and, although we were a million miles apart, he was very much at ease in my world. In fact, my friends used to say how much they enjoyed his company. Anyway, we married and were relatively happy for a while. Vivien was born and, shortly after, everything came crashing down when Donald was arrested and charged with attempted murder. He told me that some stranger attacked him in a pub because he was talking to his wife. Complete lies of course. He was sleeping with this woman, and she was going to have his child. The husband forced the truth from her, and then told him that she and Donald were going to start a new life together. He attacked Donald but bit off a bit more than he could chew and was beaten so badly that he lost the sight of one eye. There were witnesses who came forward to say that Donald acted in self-defense. So even with the level of violence, the police were forced to reduce the charge to grievous bodily harm. He was sentenced to four years, and I divorced him straight away, reverted to my maiden name of Hellman and got on with my life. When he was released, he pleaded with me to give him another chance, but by then I had no feelings for him but disgust and I told him to leave me alone. After that, he began to badger me and finally I was forced to take out an injunction against him. He would still turn up drunk at my apartment insisting to see Vivien, then thankfully he was sent to prison again for seven years following another vicious assault. About a year later, I married Arthur and finally put the horror that was Donald Sangster behind me once and for all.'

Parrot smiled as sympathetically as he knew how and said, 'Thank you, Lady Marjorie, for your candor; I know that wasn't easy for you but you have been a great help.

'That's quite alright, Chief Inspector. Are you any nearer to making an arrest?'

'We are making good progress, Lady Marjorie. The pieces are beginning to fit together. Oh, and by the way, do you have any other properties in London?'

'Yes, I have an apartment that I bought after my divorce.'

'Do you use it very often?'

'No, I haven't been there for years.'

'Is the apartment rented?'

'Probably, but you should talk to Vivien. I gave the place to her about three years ago to use when she was in town; I said that she should rent it out for some extra income. Like most youngsters, she was continually complaining about her lack of money.'

'Well, thank you again, Lady Marjorie. Is Ms Vivien at home?'

'I saw her about an hour ago in the sitting room; she was waiting for the Reynolds boy to arrive.'

The two policemen headed for the sitting room and Parrot said, 'Are you thinking what I'm thinking sergeant?'

'You mean the father and the daughter, Sir?'

'That's right; methinks they're in it together.'

Vivien Hellman's raised voice caused Parrot and Sweeney to pause outside the sitting room. Parrot quietly opened the door and clearly heard her say, 'See you at eight and don't panic.'

Parrot and Sweeney entered the room, prompting her to scream at them, 'Don't you people ever knock?' Parrot half smiled, then said, 'Sorry, Ms Hellman, but we need an urgent word with you, but please finish your conversation, we'll wait.'

'I have finished, now what do you want?'

'Who were you telling not to panic?'

'My word, what big ears we've got, If you must know I was talking to a friend of mine, she's freaking out about an exam she's taking next week.'

'She's very lucky to have such a stalwart friend. Someone who's prepared to meet up at short notice, despite the fact that her boyfriend has driven fifty miles to be with her.'

'Duncan is having dinner with his father this evening, Chief Inspector, so I was at a loose end anyway.'

My word, this girl really thinks on her feet, thought Parrot.

'Would you mind telling me the name and telephone number of your friend, Ms Hellman?'

'Yes I would; it's a private matter and doesn't concern the police.'

'Oh, but you see it does, and your reluctance to comply with a simple request is suspicious enough for me to formally interview you at the incident room. Bring her along, Sergeant.'

'Alright, you win; it wasn't a friend but it was personal.'

'Just tell me who you were having the conversation with and that will be an end to the matter.'

'I was talking to my father. He was released from prison a little while ago and he's having a tough time readjusting. I have tried to be supportive since he came out, but I'm fighting a losing battle at the moment. I was telling him not to panic because he's very down and was talking about ending it all.'

'Where are you meeting him tonight?'

'At a pub called The Grapes, about five miles from here.'

'I believe you have been putting your father up at your London apartment for the last few months.'

'Yes that's right, couldn't deny him a roof over his head, no matter what he's done.'

'Very commendable, Ms Hellman, and when did you first hit on the idea of getting your father to murder your stepfather?'

'That's ludicrous. What earthly reason would I have for killing him?'

'The oldest reason in the world, monetary gain. With Sir Arthur dead, your mother stood to inherit a fortune, some of which you figured would be heading your way. Maybe all of it if you could persuade your father to carry out one more murder.'

'You really are in fantasy land, Chief Inspector.'

'Am I, Ms Hellman? I think not. I suspect that you harbored the idea for some time, and I also suspect that Duncan Reynolds' drunken account of the wrong-doing inflicted on his father by Sir Arthur was the catalyst for you to put the plan into operation, a plan that, I might add, now contained the added ingredient of throwing suspicion over the Reynolds family. I'm sure that when we check prison records, it will show that your visits to your father coincided with the beginning of your relationship with Duncan Reynolds. The comfort and affection you heaped on a broken man camouflaged your real intention of getting him to murder your stepfather. What nasty stories you invented about Sir Arthur, we'll never know, but they found their mark and a fine man met a premature death because of your greed. I can tell you that your evil scheme was in vain, because your mother inherits very little from Sir Arthur's will. Which I suppose is what they call irony. Take her to the station, Sergeant, and formally charge her with conspiracy to murder. Just get her out of my sight.'

Parrot needed some fresh air, so he decided to take a walk in the grounds. On his way, he was waylaid by Marjorie Messenger who demanded to know why her daughter had been arrested.

'This is going to be tough on you, Lady Marjorie, but your daughter is being charged with conspiracy to murder Sir Arthur; her accomplice and the actual murderer is her father and your ex-husband, Donald Sangster, who we shall be arresting this evening.'

'Have you any proof, Chief Inspector?'

'I'm sorry, but that is a police matter. Though I can tell you that I believe your daughter to be the driving force behind the murder. I'm sorry to cause you such distress, Lady Marjorie, I truly am.'

Suddenly she began to laugh, softly at first, and then gradually, the laugh turned into a bellow, then into a pitiful whining. Parrot was bemused; he never expected this from her and did his best to calm her down.

'I'm so sorry Mr Parrot, what must you think of me. Let's take a stroll. I want to tell you something I've never told a soul.'

They walked in silence to the great lawn, where she sat down under the great chestnut tree. She composed herself and said, 'Vivien is not Donald Sangster's daughter, Chief Inspector. I told you that I found out about his philandering ways at a later stage. Well, that wasn't true. I knew from the beginning, but what he didn't know is that I was in love with a married man whom I was seeing at the same time as I was going out with Donald. Even after we got married, I continued to see him and deliberately got myself pregnant. I was terribly unhappy, and I thought if I told him I was going to have his child, he would leave his wife to be with me. Needless to say, that did not happen; he said that he couldn't see me anymore and made it clear that he loved his wife and was not prepared to leave her. So I tried to make the best of it with Donald and, when Vivien was born, things between us did improve for a short while, then they quickly went downhill and the rest you know.'

I'm so sorry, Lady Marjorie; do you have some friends to stay with? I fear the next few days are going to be very harrowing around here.'

'Yes, I think that may be for the best. May I see Vivien before I leave?'

'I'll arrange for you to see her some time tomorrow afternoon.'

'Thank you, Mr Parrot, that's very good of you and much appreciated.'

Parrot and Lady Marjorie walked back to the castle in silence before he took his leave and drove to the station where Sweeney told him that Vivien Hellman had been charged but was saying nothing.

'That doesn't concern me in the slightest; what does concern me is that we pick up Sangster this evening. No foul ups, please, Sergeant.'

Parrot needn't have worried; Sangster was swiftly arrested as he set foot in the pub and offered no resistance. He was brought to the station where he was cautioned and formally held on suspicion of the murder of Sir Arthur Messenger. Parrot and Sweeney entered the interview room and were both astonished to see a pitiful old man before them. Time and prison had not been kind to Donald Sangster, his dark sunken eyes and sallow complexion, together with his disheveled appearance, made it difficult to imagine that sitting before the two policemen was a person of menace.

Parrot sat down and said, 'Is there anything we can get you, Mr Sangster, a hot drink or a sandwich maybe?'

Sangster raised his head slightly. 'Cut the kindness crap,' he said in a low rasping voice. 'I've heard it all before, just get on with it.'

'Alright,' said Parrot. 'Let's do that. I'm told you have waived your right to legal counsel, is that correct?'

'No interest in those bloodsuckers; they're worse than coppers.'

'You understand that this interview is being recorded and a transcript may be used against you in court.'

'Stop farting about can't you. Just ask me what you want?'

'Very well. Why did you kill Sir Arthur Messenger?'

'Because he was a fake. Everyone kept saying what a good bloke he was. But I knew different.'

'In what way did you know, Mr Sangster?'

'My Vivien told me what a nasty toad he really was. Stealing other people's ideas and passing them off as his own and how he used to touch her when she was young.'

'Are you telling me that Sir Arthur sexually interfered with his stepchild?'

'Ask Vivien, she'll tell you.'

'You think a lot of Vivien don't you?'

'She's class, looked after me a treat. When I got out, I had nothing, no friends, no money, and nowhere to stay; she's been like an angel to me these past months.'

'When did she start to visit you in prison?'

'About a year ago.'

'Didn't it strike you as strange that she turned up one day out of the blue?'

'She wanted to come before, but Marjorie told her not to, and that bastard Messenger said that he would cut off her allowance if she disobeyed her mother.'

'So when did you and Vivien start to plan to kill Sir Arthur?'

'Vivien's not involved in this. I decided to kill him the day she told me about being molested.'

'So, you drove down here in the early hours of the morning. You parked up. Then walked through the forest, laid in wait for your target, and then coldly shot him with a titanium bolt?'

'That's about right.

'Had you been to the castle before?'

'No, first time.'

'So how did you know that Sir Arthur would be at the exact spot where you were waiting?'

'I didn't, that was pure chance. If he hadn't have turned up, I would have kept trying until he did.'

'Do you seriously expect us to believe that you acted alone; you have been set up a treat by your angel of mercy, Mr Sangster. She has sown every vicious seed of hate in your mind, but then again how could you possibly question someone who had shown you such compassion? Add the fact that she happens to be your daughter and you never had a chance, you poor chump.'

Parrot got up and suspended the interview. 'Come on Sweeney; let's talk to his little angel. Oh, and by the way, Mr Sangster, you might like to know that Vivien Hellman is not actually your daughter.'

'What are you talking about? Is this some kind of trick to make me squeal on my Vivien?'

'No trick, I can assure you. It is the bona fide truth and came from Lady Marjorie's own lips this afternoon.'

'Then she's lying.'

'I don't think so; she had no reason to and, besides, have you never thought about the distinct lack of facial and physical similarity between yourself and Vivien? Something to ponder over till we return.'

Sweeney turned to Parrot as they left the room. 'Are you going to tell Vivien that Sangster's not her father, Sir?'

'No, I'll leave that to her mother. She's coming over tomorrow afternoon. You know, Sweeney; this conspiracy charge against her is going to be very difficult to prove if Sangster doesn't change his story.'

'Is that the reason you told Sangster he wasn't her father?'

'You bet your life it was; not my finest moment but we're dealing with a particularly nasty piece of work in Vivien Hellman.'

They entered the room to find Vivien Hellman accompanied by her lawyer. Parrot, over the course of a long career had dealt with just about every type of criminal, from gutter life to the landed gentry, but somehow he found this young girl among the most odious. He decided to let Sweeney commence the questioning.

'Ms Hellman we have reason to believe that you were complicit in the murder of your stepfather by means of deception and planning.'

'Really, Sergeant, I haven't the foggiest idea what you're talking about.'

'We have charged your father with Sir Arthur's murder; apparently he's under the impression that you were sexually molested by your stepfather when you were a child, is that true?'

'No of course not. I may have said that I didn't like him touching and kissing me when I was a young but that was because he always smelt of tobacco and whiskey.'

'Did you tell your father that Sir Arthur plagiarized Duncan Reynolds story and turned it into *The Dove Dynasty* and was it your idea to kill him with a bolt from a crossbow, thus throwing suspicion on the Reynolds family?'

Her lawyer put a hand on his client's arm and said, 'No need to answer that, Ms Hellman. Pure speculation, Sergeant. If this line of questioning is a sample of your evidence against my client, then I suggest you drop the charges before I file a claim for wrongful arrest.'

The door opened and a constable beckoned to Parrot and then whispered, 'Sangster wants to see you, Sir.'

'Sergeant, suspend this interview. It seems Mr Sangster has requested our presence.' The look of concern on Vivien Hellman's face pleased Parrot no end. As soon as the policeman returned, Sangster said, 'I've never pleaded for anything in my life, but I beg you now to tell me if you were telling the truth about Vivien not being my kid.'

'Mr Sangster, I told you the truth; she's not your child and I'm telling you the truth now when I say that you have been systematically manipulated by an evil young woman. She took advantage of your situation by offering affection when you had none. She endeared herself to you, to the extent where your gratitude had no limits, and she waited until the time was ripe to carry out her plan to murder a fine and honorable man, using you as the potential fall guy should anything go wrong. Look, you know the score here Sangster; you're going down for a long time, but there are extenuating circumstances which, at the very least, will show that you were used as a pawn in a much bigger game by an unimaginably cold-hearted woman.'

Sangster nodded, then said, 'Ok, you've been fair to me; I'll tell you everything.'

For the next hour, he gave Parrot and Sweeney everything they needed to charge Vivien Hellman with conspiracy to commit murder. When he had finished, Parrot asked him, 'Would you have admitted to Vivien's involvement if she had been your daughter?'

'Of course not, but she's not my flesh and blood, and I don't care what happens to her now.'

As the two policemen left the station, Sweeney said, 'What a bloody awful case, Sir, so many lives in tatters for one person's greed.'

'Not just one person's, Sergeant, don't forget the mother in all this; she wasn't exactly a role model, but don't be too downhearted, Sergeant; it's not all gloom and doom.'

'What do you mean, Sir?'

'Well, Martin Reynolds and Gwen Silsbury are getting married, Duncan Reynolds has had a lucky escape, and the Messenger family will continue to train aspiring writers in accordance with Sir Arthur's wishes.'

'That's an extremely positive attitude, Sir.'

'You need one in this business, along with an understanding partner who can cook. Nothing quite like going home to a loving wife, a good meal, and a glass of wine, to banish the cares of the day. There's something for you to work on Daniel.'

The Poacher's Last Shot

Detective Chief Inspector George Parrot's idea of a perfect Saturday morning consists of a full English breakfast accompanied by two mugs of tea. The second of which he takes into his conservatory with the morning newspaper. He relaxes in his favorite armchair, which affords him the best view of his well stocked, colorful garden, and is the epitome of a contented man. He briefly reads the paper's national and world events and flits through the sports pages before having a stab at the cryptic crossword and revels in one of life's great pleasures, namely peace and quiet, which if asked, he would tell you ranks alongside his lifelong love affair with most things edible. Audrey Parrot, as usual had arranged to pick up their eldest daughter Jenny and, safe in the knowledge that lunch, plus shopping, plus afternoon coffee, plus of course chatting, should equal at least five hours, he sighs the sigh of a man luxuriating in his own company and surroundings. In addition, he had already factored in a stroll to The Feathers, his local pub, for a couple of pints of his favorite ale, which only served to heighten his already buoyant mood.

Unfortunately for Parrot on this particular Saturday morning, events were unfolding elsewhere that would combine to disrupt the equilibrium of his day. The first rumblings appeared when he heard the front door open unexpectedly and then, finding Audrey, Jenny, and his younger daughter Sarah in the hallway.

'Well, this is a nice surprise,' Parrot said warmly, dreading the bad news that he knew was about to unfold.

'Go into the kitchen, girls, and make a pot of coffee, while I speak to your father,' Audrey said. *It definitely is bad news*, thought Parrot. *My daughters shunted off to make coffee and Audrey wants to speak to their father, not talk to their dad.*

She ushered him back into the conservatory and said, 'Sarah was at Jenny's when I arrived, and she's very upset, so I brought her back here so I could talk to her.'

'I assume that the "I" means us?' Parrot said.

'Yes of course; please don't be awkward, George. Sarah needs our time and our advice.'

'What's happened to upset her so much?'

'She's had a blazing row with Mark and he didn't come home last night.'

'Do you know what the row was about?'

'Yes, but I want Sarah to tell you in her own words.'

'Fair enough. Let's go into the kitchen then.'

'No, wait for the girls to bring the coffee out here; then we can all be more comfortable,' said Audrey.

As with most people, Parrot hated hanging around to hear bad news but did his best to wait patiently and made a concerted effort not to fidget. After a couple of minutes, Jenny and Sarah reappeared with the coffee, and although it wasn't exactly the liquid refreshment he had in mind, he smiled broadly and thanked them.

'Sorry to ruin your Saturday, Dad,' said Sarah.

'Don't give it a second thought; you know that the two of you and your mum take precedence over anything, let alone my precious Saturdays. Now, come on Sarah, what's this all about?'

'Mark and I had a terrible fight and then he stormed out and didn't come home last night,' Sarah said in tears.

'Can you tell me what you fought about?'

'I told him that I would like to start a family, and he just exploded at me.'

'That doesn't sound like Mark. What exactly did he say?'

'He said that I was crazy to even think about it at the moment and told me to get the idea out of my head, but it was the way he said it. He was so angry, then I got angry, and then suddenly he was gone. It's so unlike him, Dad. Will you please talk to him?'

'Sarah, my darling, you know that's not a very good idea. The pair of you need to sort this out yourselves. I'm sure you will. Without taking sides, I tend to agree with Mark.' The comment provoked a stern look from Audrey, but, undeterred, Parrot continued, 'Look, you're twenty-two, and Mark's a couple of years older. You both have good jobs and have a lifestyle that many other young couples can only dream about, so what's the big hurry? You can enjoy your life together for a few more years, and then consider having children, and I say that as someone who can't wait for another grandchild. I know I speak for your mum as well.'

'I'm not sure I want to have children with him now, anyway,' said Sarah.

'Oh come on, darling, you don't mean that?' said Audrey.

'Sarah, how often do you visit Jenny?' said Parrot, trying not to sound like a chief inspector.

'I don't know, two or three times a week, why?'

'Because you go there and see Jenny and Trevor playing happy families with little Michael, and everything seems so complete, and it's natural for you to want the same, am I right?'

Sarah smiled through her tears and said, 'Yes Dad, you are right, but there's nothing wrong in feeling like that, is there?'

'Absolutely not, but I suggest you talk to your sister about the whole package. She may well provide you with some valuable insight.'

This brought an informed look from Jenny, who said, 'I wouldn't swap my life for anything, but, if I'm totally honest, there are times I wished Trevor and I had spent a couple of extra years as a couple.'

The phone rang, and Parrot got up to answer it, grateful to have a slight diversion. He came back after a couple of minutes with a look Audrey spotted immediately, that prompted her to say, 'Oh no, George, tell me you don't have to go out.'

'I'm sorry, everyone…shouldn't be more than an hour.'

Parrot waved to his family as he drove off, then parked his car around the next corner and continued his journey on foot to his destination.

Entering the Feathers, he spotted Mark Walters, his son-in-law, at the bar wearing a welcoming smile of gratitude.

'Thanks so much for coming, George. I really need to talk to you.'

'For the price of a pint, my boy, you will have my full and undivided attention.'

'Sarah's obviously told you about our bust up last night.'

'Yes, she's back at our place with her mum and sister.'

'Yes, I know. Trevor told me earlier when I rang. Look, I realize that I was totally out of order not to go home last night.'

'Yes, you totally were,' Parrot interrupted. 'Whatever the reason for the argument, never stay out all night. No matter how you're feeling. Apart from being a juvenile act, it, causes unnecessary worry to other people.' He paused for a couple of seconds after seeing the admonished look on Mark's face, then continued, 'Something's not right at work, am I right?'

Mark made a noise, somewhere between a sigh and a laugh, and then said, 'You know, George, ever since I've known Sarah, she has said how impossible it is to keep anything from you, not for long anyway, and now I see what she meant. And yes, you are right; work is a problem for me at the moment.'

'Is your job under threat?' said Parrot.

'That's the worse part. Not knowing for sure is making me more edgy. My boss called me in about three months ago and said cutbacks were being discussed at head office, and, while he didn't think I would be affected, he couldn't be sure and suggested I should start to look around as a precaution. So you can understand why I went off the deep end at Sarah yesterday.'

'Yes, I understand, Mark; believe me, I really do. Uncertainty eats away at you...especially financial uncertainty. I know, I've been there, and I can tell you that it's not a place to be on your own. You should have shared your concerns with Sarah and avoided what happened last night.'

'I didn't want to worry her, George.'

'A noble but flawed sentiment, Mark. A real partnership is about trust and confidence in one another, and I guarantee that when you tell her later today, as I'm sure you're going to, that weight you've been carrying won't seem half as heavy. So, you can buy me another pint and then pick up my daughter. I suggest that after you've cleared the air, you take her somewhere special for dinner. Nothing seems that bad after some good food and a glass or two of wine. And remember: whatever happens, face it together.'

Mark left the bar after thanking his father-in-law profusely and promising to keep their conversation strictly between the two of them. Parrot quietly sipped his favorite ale and thought the day was not lost after all. He waited long enough for Mark to have collected Sarah, then slowly strolled back home. Audrey's car was not in the driveway, and Parrot assumed she was driving Jenny home, an assumption that was to be proven wrong as soon as he read her note on the kitchen table.

Dear George,

Jenny and I are going to the Mall for a couple of hours to do some shopping; we will probably just have a light snack. So while you relax this afternoon, you may like to think where you are taking me for dinner this evening. I do hope you didn't drink too much beer in The Feathers, when

you met Mark. At least the boy had enough sense to call and ask your advice.
Love Audrey.

Parrot smiled and thought to himself what a very lucky man he was to have met and married his perfect soul mate. With that in mind, he decided to give some thought for a suitable venue for dinner. And what better way to contemplate an evening meal than with a lunchtime one, he thought. So, five minutes later, he returned to his armchair with a plateful of mature cheddar cheese, two wedges of a seedy loaf, and a jar of crispy pickled onions and resumed his at-peace-with-the-world disposition. He was halfway through his gastronomic treat when the phone rang. For a brief moment, he considered not answering. He dismissed the thought, then wished he hadn't when he heard the voice of Detective Sergeant Daniel Sweeney.

'Sorry about this, Sir, but there's been a murder over at Woodcote Lodge.'

'Isn't that the place that's just been bought by Justin Brett the England footballer.'

'Yes, Sir, and it appears he's the victim.'

'Where are you now, Sergeant?'

'I'm on my way over there, Sir.'

'Well, make a detour and pick me up would you?'

'Right you are, Sir; be with you in ten minutes.'

Parrot scribbled a note for Audrey, then returned to finish his interrupted lunch, by which time Sweeney had arrived.

'So, Sergeant, what do we know?' said Parrot.

'Well, the station got a call about half an hour ago from Brett's girlfriend. She was in a bit of a state, seems she found his body in the bedroom. Judging from her manner over the phone, it wasn't a pretty sight.'

'She's a famous model, isn't she? Mandy something or other?'

'Yes, her name is Mandy Summers,' *as if you didn't know*, thought Sweeney. 'You may have seen her in the dailies, Sir.'

'Not the sort of dailies I read, Sergeant. Does she pose topless?' asked Parrot casually.

'Topless in the tabloids and everything on show for certain magazines, Sir,' said Sweeney in a very matter-of-fact manner.

'Anyone else staying at the house?'

'Yes, Sir, although Ms Summers said that she only arrived this morning. Apparently, Justin Brett threw a party last night and I gather there are a lot of overnight guests still hanging around.'

'Well, let's hope they've not been hanging around the crime scene, Sergeant,' said Parrot sardonically. 'Did you get in touch with Dr. Starkey?'

'Yes, Sir, and he was none too pleased; he was just off to town with his wife when I rang.'

'If I know Dr. Harry Starkey, which I do very well, his displeasure was for the sole benefit of his wife. Inside, he was turning cartwheels...believe me, he hates shopping more than I do,' Parrot said, laughing aloud.

'I also managed to find four uniformed officers, Sir. I thought we could station a couple of them outside the Lodge, and we can use the other two to take statements.'

'Well done, Sergeant, but when news of Justin Brett's murder leaks out, and it will very shortly, we're going to need a lot more manpower at the front gate. I'll call the chief constable. I'm sure he will use his influence when I tell him the name of the victim,' Parrot said with more than a hint of sarcasm.

The two detectives arrived at Woodcote Lodge and, as Parrot had predicted, word had already spread about the footballer's demise, evidenced by a small gathering of local reporters that Parrot recognized outside the gates to the lodge. 'How the hell do they get wind of events so quickly?' said Sweeney.

'Who knows? There's always someone around after fast money. Could be the cleaner, or a neighbor, or perhaps even one of the guests. It's become a nasty part of today's culture, if indeed you can call it that, but as long as the media persists to pay handsomely for seemingly any type of scandal, gossip, or actual photographs involving real or supposed celebrities, I guess it will continue to flourish for as long as the public maintain an insatiable appetite for such unadulterated trivial rubbish.'

As they drove along the winding driveway to the Lodge, Sweeney said, 'I read that Justin Brett planned to build a helipad and a five a side football pitch on the back lawn of the Lodge.'

'Why am I not surprised? Footballers earn obscene amounts of money for what they do; they ought to have their salaries capped.'

'Can't do that, Sir. We live in a free market society these days.'

'Well, in that case, the free market society has a bloody lot to answer for.'

'I agree, but it's still the best system we have, better for people to be overpaid and free than underpaid and oppressed.'

'Quite right, Sweeney, I stand corrected. I never realized that you were a student of political and economic history, or is it humanism?'

'A bit of each actually, Sir, but you know it does amaze me how some people take our modern lifestyle for granted.'

'It shouldn't do. Every generation is at odds with the previous one in some shape or form, just a question of degree. Although I have to say that what completely baffles me is this generation's obsession with reality shows. A friend of mine told me that his seventeen-year-old son was watching television late one night, and, when he went to say goodnight to him, he realized there was no sound coming from the program. He thought the boy must have pressed the mute button, but no, he was and had been sitting there watching a group of people who were fast asleep in a dormitory, while a hidden camera monitored their total lack of consciousness. Now that's what I call a generation gap. Anyway, enough of the amateur fish and chip shop philosophy; we've got a murder to solve.'

Police Constable Malcolm 'Spider' Webb greeted Parrot and Sweeney and said, 'Dr. Starkey and his team have just arrived, Sir, and I've moved all the guests into the main lounge.'

'How many of them are there?' asked Sweeney.

'Nine in total, four men and five women. Some of them are pretty hung over. Apart from Mandy Summers, must have been quite a party the poacher threw last night, Sir.'

'What do you mean by poacher, constable?' asked Parrot.

'That was Justin Brett's nickname, Sir. He wasn't the most talented player you'll ever see, and a lot of people said he was lazy and didn't work hard enough for the team, but, when it came to scoring goals, wow, he just came alive in the penalty area. All the experts reckoned he was the quickest player over five yards they had ever seen.'

'We used to call that type of player a goal hanger when I was young,' said Parrot, which brought about quizzical looks between Sweeney and Webb about their boss's, 'Jumpers for Goalposts' moment.

'So, Constable Webb, who exactly have you corralled into the lounge?'

'Right, Sir, there's Justin Brett's agent Jack Peacock and his wife Janice. Then, three of his club teammates, Johnny Buckland, Terry Maguire, and Mick Harmer. Buckland and Maguire are with their wives, and Harmer is with his fiancé, as she was at pains to point out.'

'Well done, Constable. Sweeney and I will interview Ms Summers first, and then we'll see the agent and his wife. Webb, you and the other constables take statements from the rest. Oh, and get me a list of everyone at the party last night. Before I forget, I'd better have a word with Dr. Starkey. Back in five minutes.' Entering the master bedroom and finding the doctor hunched over the body of the dead footballer, Parrot chirped, 'Well, this beats Saturday afternoon shopping with the missus, eh, Harry?'

'Not funny, George. I was a big fan of his. Best goal scorer this country's unearthed for ages. Somebody didn't care too much about our chances in the next World Cup.'

'Anything for me before I start asking questions?'

'He's been dead between nine to twelve hours; skull's been repeatedly beaten and crushed by one of his own golden boots. By my reckoning, he's won the top goal scorer award for the last three years, so you might want to check to see if the other two are here somewhere,' Starkey said, pointing to the bloodstained object laying on a pillow at the foot of the bed. 'Strange thing to do, George, looks as though the killer placed it there deliberately to say look at my handiwork and now give me the prize.'

'Struck me like that too, Harry; of course the killer could have thrown it on to the bed and it just happened to land like that, but it looks like the pillow has been puffed up, and the placement of the boot has a symmetry that suggests it was put there methodically for all to see.'

'Very theatrical gesture, George?'

'Maybe the killer believes he deserves an award, you know like a reward for a public service.'

'Justin Brett was a football player, not a gangster, a murderer, or a pedophile,' said the doctor.

'Quite right, Harry, but who knows what we may uncover about him, when we start the investigation,' said Parrot breaking into a Machiavellian grin.

'I tell you what is puzzling me though; there are no bloodstains on the bed, and why is his body on the floor?' I mean, why would the killer throw him off the bed then strike him?'

Sweeney was waiting in the study with Mandy Summers as Parrot entered the room. He introduced himself and apologized for keeping her waiting, then said, 'I understand that this must be very difficult for you, but I'm sure you appreciate our need to question you, especially as you discovered the body.'

'Yes of course, Chief Inspector. What do you want to know?' she said in a rich, deep tone, which caught Parrot completely off guard, as it had his sergeant five minutes earlier.

'It's a normal reaction, Mr Parrot. Blonde women who take their clothes off for a living are not supposed to be well spoken; that's the stereotypical view, wouldn't you say?' she said, throwing the ball firmly into his court.

'I do apologize if my reaction offended you, Ms Summers,' said Parrot, then moving on swiftly, he said, 'Now, could you tell me what time you arrived at the lodge this morning?'

'I got here around noon and let myself in with the key Justin kept under the bay tree pot on the left-hand side of the front door. I went into the kitchen for a glass of juice and briefly spoke to Jack and Janice Peacock, who were having a late breakfast. Then, I went to the bedroom and found Justin.'

'Did you touch anything in the bedroom?'

'No, I screamed and ran straight out.'

'Did anyone else go into the bedroom to your knowledge?'

'Jack and Janice must have heard my scream. They rushed up the stairs, and I told them what had happened, then Jack went into the bedroom, and

Janice took me downstairs and poured me a glass of water.'

'How long would you say Mr Peacock was in the bedroom?'

'Not very long…a couple of minutes at most. Then, he came down and he looked as though he'd been crying; then, he told me to call the police.'

'Why didn't Mr Peacock make the call? He must have seen you were distressed.'

'I did ask him to, but he said it would probably be better for me to ring, as I had found the body.'

'And did Mrs Peacock remain with you downstairs throughout this time?'

'After she gave me the drink, she went upstairs and came down again a few seconds before Jack.'

'Did you see or talk to anyone other than the Peacocks between arriving and going to the bedroom?'

'Yes, Jackie Buckland and Brenda Maguire passed through the kitchen and went into the garden.'

'Did you speak to them?'

'Very briefly. Jackie said that I'd missed a good thrash, and they needed some fresh air. They both looked extremely hung over.'

'Now, I want you to think back to when you entered the bedroom. Did you notice an object on the bed?'

Mandy Summers thought hard and then replied, 'I seem to remember seeing one of Justin's golden football boots at the foot of the bed. Was that the murder weapon?'

'We don't know for sure yet,' said Parrot. 'Was there anything unusual about the position of the boot?'

Again, she thought hard for a few seconds before replying, 'I don't think so, but I didn't take a great deal of notice. After seeing Justin, I began to feel sick and rushed from the room…it was just a fleeting glimpse.'

'Why were you not at the party last night?'

'There was an all-day fashion shoot in London, and I had arranged to have dinner with a few old friends.'

'Were these friends of yours at the shoot?'

'No. I met them afterwards, old school friends actually; there's still a few of them that are prepared to associate with the "fallen angel" as I'm known in certain circles, but I'm not invited back for school reunions anymore, and I certainly don't get invited back to give the girls a talk on career choices.'

'Is Mandy Summers your real name?' asked Sweeney.

'It's Amanda actually, but Janice thought Mandy Summers sounded sluttier and more appealing for my line of work.'

'How is Janice Peacock involved with your career?' asked Parrot.

'Oh, I thought you knew…she's been my agent for the last five years. It was at one of the Peacocks' gatherings that I met Justin.'

'How long had the two of you been seeing each other?'

'Off and on for about a year. More off than on recently.'

'So it wasn't a serious relationship?'

'It was never meant to be, Mr Parrot. To be perfectly honest, I think Justin liked having me around mainly because I have a plummy voice; it somehow gave him credibility. He was always more concerned what people thought and wrote about him than he needed to be, but I suppose that's what's called insecurity. He had a pretty rough upbringing. He was an unwanted child, you know, and he told me that his mother had never shown him any love or affection as a kid...probably explained his craving for acceptance.'

'So your relationship with Justin Brett was not exclusive?' asked Sweeney.

'It was exclusive but not serious on my part and not exclusive but serious on a friendship level on his, if that makes any sense.'

'So he was seeing other women?' Sweeney said.

'He couldn't help himself. I personally think that he used women in an effort to purge himself of his loveless mother. For all his bravado, especially with his teammates, I actually saw him as a rather sad and lonely person.'

'So would you say that you were good friends?' asked Parrot.

'We became very good friends. At first, it was purely physical, but, for some time now, we've met up purely platonically.'

'So you didn't come here for a romantic weekend then?'

'No. As a matter of fact, he asked me to come down today because he said that he needed to talk to me... and before you ask, he didn't say what about.'

'So all this talk in the tabloid press about the two of you getting married is incorrect?' asked Sweeney.

'Totally incorrect. It is just their usual frivolous speculation to fill their tawdry pages.'

'Do you know if anyone else knew about the key under the plant pot?' asked Parrot.

'I can't say for sure, but I would imagine so. Justin was the least security conscious person I've ever met. He had a state-of-the-art security system installed on police advice, but I never saw him lock a door or set an alarm.

'You mentioned earlier that Justin was seeing other women. Can you give us any of their names?'

'Not specifically. Look, Mr Parrot, the guy just couldn't say no; he was on a constant ego trip; he told me as much, and that was the reason I stopped sleeping with him. I still liked him…he could still be good fun, but the more successful he was, the more insecure and intense he became, and the less fun we had.'

'Are you able to throw any light on why he was murdered? Anything at all at this early stage would be invaluable,' said Parrot.

'I'm sorry, I can't think of any reason why anyone would kill him. He wasn't particularly popular with a few of his teammates. He said they were just jealous because he earned more and played for his country, but it wasn't a major issue for him.'

'Has there been any talk, or any rumors even, of him being involved with any of his teammates' wives?' Parrot probed gently.

'I don't get involved in gossip or rumor mongering, Chief Inspector, but I'm sure when you interview them, they will prove to be a mine of information on that subject.'

'Just a couple more questions, Ms Summers, and then you can go for the time being,' Parrot said with a smile. 'Did Justin have a drink or drugs problem?'

'Absolutely not. Like me, he never touched either, except for the occasional sleeping tablet. He was extremely careful about what he ate and drank; keeping fit with him was an obsession. I've woken up in the middle of the night to find him, legs curled under the bed, in the middle of two hundred situps. If he did have an addiction, it was to those fizzy sports drinks. He used to get through ten cans or more of those a day.'

'Just as a matter of interest, did you always have it in mind to be a model?'

'Not in the slightest. I was studying drama at college when, by chance, I met a celebrated photographer who persuaded me to pose, fully clothed, I might add. Anyway, he sent the photos to one of the tabloids and, suddenly, hey, presto, I had arrived. I still have it in mind to finish the drama course one day, and I would love to work in the theatre, but the reality is that I just don't have the time at the moment, and I really enjoy my job and the lifestyle it affords me. I get to travel to great locations and meet interesting people, and they pay me ludicrous sums of money for the privilege.'

'How did your parents react to your chosen profession?'

'Mum was fine. She did a bit of modeling when she was young, and she's very open-minded. Dad, on the other hand, was very upset. He said he didn't mind his daughter modeling clothes and swimwear, but he didn't like the idea of people seeing me nude. An understandable reaction, I suppose.'

'Just two more questions,' Parrot said. 'Where did you stay last night, and did you drive here this morning?'

'I stayed at a friend's apartment in London, and we both slept in this morning, after quite a late night. She made me some breakfast, and we chatted for a while, then I drove here about ten forty-five.'

'Thank you very much, Ms Summers, that's all for now. If you could let me have the names, addresses, and telephone numbers of your two old school friends, I'd be most grateful.'

'Yes, of course. I'll go and write them down for you straight away,' Mandy Summers said, and then she stood up and walked slowly and very gracefully from the room.

Sweeney looked at his boss and said, 'Well, Sir, what's your opinion of Mandy Summers?'

'A very intelligent and attractive young lady, Sergeant, and I think she may have more to tell us. One thing she mentioned about Brett being a fitness fanatic could well explain why he was laying on the floor of his bedroom.'

'How do you mean, Sir?' asked Sweeney.

'He could have started exercising and then fallen asleep, especially if someone had slipped something into one of those energy drinks he was so partial to.'

'Do you think she could be the killer, Sir?'

'Can't rule her out completely. After all, she could have driven here in the middle of the night, let herself in, then quietly crept into the bedroom and bashed his head in before heading back to her friend's apartment, but, if it turns out that Brett was drugged, then that makes the murder premeditated, and she's in the clear.'

'Shall I ask Jack Peacock to come in, Sir?'

'Bring him here in about ten minutes, Sweeney. I need to make a couple of phone calls. While I'm making them, go and have a look at the crime scene and see if Dr. Starkey has anything new for us.'

Parrot first called Chief Constable Oswald Rowley to ask for more uniformed officers from nearby stations to guard the entrances to the Lodge, a request that was immediately granted, as he knew it would be, given Rowley's fondness for high-profile cases. Then, he called Audrey to say that he couldn't promise to take her out for dinner that evening. As usual, she said in an even tone that she understood but did ask him to try extra hard, as Sarah and Mark had managed to book a table for the four of them, by way of a thank you at The Crooked Chimney, the Parrots' favorite restaurant. If ever there was an incentive designed to galvanize George Parrot's maximum effort level, then indeed this was the incentive.

Sweeney returned to the study with Jack Peacock and introduced Parrot, who then said, 'I believe you were Justin Brett's sole business agent, Mr Peacock, is that correct?'

'Yeah, that's right. I've looked after the boy's interests for just over seven years, ever since he signed professional forms as a seventeen-year-old,' said Peacock, in a broad cockney accent. 'England has lost a great talent today, Mr Parrot, a great talent,' he repeated with a pronounced sigh.

'How did you become an agent, Mr Peacock?'

'Well, I had to pack the game in about fifteen years ago, knee ligaments went for a burton for a third time, so I opened a sports agency and never looked back. Got lucky cos that's just about the time when the big money come into the top flight, yer know the TV dosh, well players wages went through the bloomin' roof overnight and the agency business went ballistic.'

'Did you approach Justin Brett?'

'No, didn't have to; me and his uncle, Johnny Brett, been best mates since we was nippers. So, Johnny and Justin's dad, Kenny, and the boy came round to my gaff one night and asked me to look after the lad. Knew I wouldn't stitch the kid up, not like some of the scheisters around at the time.'

'Do you look after the interests of any of Justin's teammates?'

'I've got Terry Maguire, Micky Harmer, and Johnny Buckland on the books, plus a couple of very promising youngsters, but Justin was my top man by streets.'

'And I believe your wife is also involved with the agency?' asked Parrot.

'Yeah, she's got her own clients, though, mainly models and TV soap actresses. Amazing the demand for those women and Jan's done great in her own right, with no help from yours truly.'

'Okay then, Mr Peacock, now I need to ask you about what happened earlier, specifically after Ms Summers screamed and you and your wife rushed upstairs,'

'Well, we both heard a scream, and when we got up the stairs, there was Mandy in a right old state. Jan took her downstairs and I went into the bedroom and saw the boy on the floor. I knew he was a goner, soon as I clocked the back of his head, terrible sight.'

'Did you touch, move, or remove anything from the room, Mr Peacock?' said Parrot in his most serious of interview voices.

'No. I bent down over Justin, put a hand on his shoulder, and just started sobbing. I couldn't help myself. I was there at his christening…I thought, now I'm gonna be there at his funeral, and then I thought what this would do to Kenny. He absolutely idolized the boy.'

'What about Justin's mother? Ms Summers told us that she was distant with her son.'

'Distant doesn't begin to describe it. If you saw the two of them together, Mr Parrot, you would never Adam and Eve they were related, let alone mother and son.'

'Does she have other children?'

'Yeah, she had two more, Robert and Alison, lovely kids.'

'How does the mother treat them?'

'Oh, she loves them to bits, used to get right up Justin's nose. That's why he moved out of the house after he signed pro forms.'

'Did you notice the golden football boot on his bed?'

'Yeah, but I didn't touch it.'

'When your wife came back up the stairs, did she go into the bedroom?'

'Only for a few seconds. I got up and took her outside.'

'Ms Summers also said that your wife came down before you. Did you go back into the bedroom?'

'Yeah, I went to the bathroom first and got a towel, and then I covered the boy's head with it. I know I shouldn't have, but I just didn't want the lad lying there like that.'

'Do you and Mrs Peacock have any children?' Parrot asked casually.

'Twin girls, Debbie and Lily, and a boy Jack junior. Great kids all three of them. Debbie's married to a smashing bloke called Andy Watts, you may have heard of him; he's a pucker sports journalist, written loads of biographies of famous athletes. Then, there's my Lily; she works with her mum at the agency, and Jack's the brainbox of the family; he's at Oxford studying law would you believe. I have to pinch meself sometimes, Mr Parrot, to think that an old dunce like me from the east end of London could have produced a genius like my Jack.'

'Is your son at Oxford at the moment?'

'No, he's back home for a few weeks.'

'Do you know if he was at yesterday's party?'

'I don't think so; he and my Lily took off together with some friends last night. Said they were going to the pub, but they could have popped in to see Justin, I suppose.'

'Well, thanks very much, Mr Peacock; you've been very helpful. That's all for now…oh, there is just one other thing. What time did you and Mrs Peacock go to bed last night?'

'Well, I don't see what that's got to do with the boy's murder, but Janice went up about half eleven, and I watched the telly till about twelve fifteen,' at which Parrot looked at Sweeney and received a vacant expression, together with a half raised hands gesture.

'Mr Peacock, am I to understand that you and your wife were not here last night at Justin Brett's party?'

'Old codgers like us, Mr Parrot, cor luv us no. We drove over this morning. We'd only just arrived before

Mandy got here and were waiting for Justin to come down.'

'So why did you drive here this morning and from where?'

'Justin called me yesterday and asked me to. He said there was something he wanted to discuss with Jan and me. We live about ten miles away in Little Compton, bought the Old Rectory there about eight or nine years ago. First, we used to come down for the odd weekend, but we both loved the place so much we decided to make it our permanent home about four years ago. Justin loved coming down when he could. Said it was his refuge. I put him onto this gaff, when it came up for sale about a year ago.'

'I suppose you want to see the missus now. Shall I send her in?'

'Not just yet. We'll call her in a few minutes. Thanks again, Mr Peacock.'

'Right you are, then. I'll tell her,' said Peacock and left the room.

Parrot and Sweeney looked at each other with raised eyebrows, then Parrot said, 'Well, Sergeant, there's a lesson for both of us: never assume, always question. Not that he is in the clear, he could have driven here in ten minutes and parked his car off the road and walked the rest of the way. Bearing in mind what Mandy Summers said about Justin's lack of security, he could easily have got into this place. I wonder what he wanted to speak to Mandy and the Peacocks about. Anyway, Sergeant, what do you make of our affable cockney friend?'

'He plays the lovable jack the lad image up for all that its worth, Sir, but I sense that he would make a very bad enemy.'

'I agree. Did you notice how he was very personal about everybody? When I asked him about children, we got their names and personnel files and the same with Justin's family, all except the mother; he never mentioned her name once, which struck me as being out of sync.'

'Maybe he just doesn't like her, Sir,' said Sweeney.

'Or maybe it's because he liked her too much, and allowing for that possibility, I want you to get a DNA sample from him and have it compared to the victim's. If he asks why, tell him that it's standard procedure when anybody has been present at the scene of a murder, and get the same tests run on his wife and Mandy Summers. After that, I want to know the financial state of his business, so bank statements and tax returns please.'

'If he is the father, then that rules him out of killing Justin, doesn't it?' Sweeney suggested.

'He may be completely unaware of the fact and could have a different motive, which rules him back in. Even if he does know, it's not totally unheard of for a father to kill a son. Right, let's see what his wife has to say for herself,' Parrot said, anxious to keep things moving along at a brisk pace with his favorite restaurant in mind.

Janice Peacock entered the study, and Parrot introduced Sweeney and himself and invited her to take a seat. He noticed immediately, as did Sweeney, that she carried herself well and seemed confident. She was tall and slim; while not classically beautiful, Parrot thought she looked very photogenic.

'Your husband tells me that you run your own part of the agency, Mrs Peacock.'

'Yes, I got involved some years ago when the children were more or less offhand,' she said in a velvety tone, not dissimilar to that of Mandy Summers.

'Forgive me,' said Parrot, 'but I couldn't help noticing how gracefully you walked in here just now. I was wondering if you had ever done any modeling.'

'I have, Chief Inspector. Believe it or not, I still do occasionally. Middle-aged photogenic women are actually quite well sought after for fashion magazines and mail order catalogues and suchlike.'

'Yes, my wife is constantly telling me that fifty is the new forty and so on.'

'She's absolutely right. Today's middle-aged women are fitter, healthier, and I might add wealthier and more independent than ever before. I have half a dozen ladies over fifty on my books, and they all are in constant demand for work.'

'Mr Peacock tells me that your youngest daughter Lily works in your office.'

'Yes, her choice entirely. She could have chosen any number of careers, and, to be quite frank, Chief Inspector, I was a little surprised, but delighted when she told me she wanted to come on board. She has expanded the business in so many directions that I could never have dreamt of.'

'And your other daughter is married to a famous sportswriter I understand?'

'Yes, they are a good match and very happy together.'

'Any grandchildren?' Parrot asked.

'Not yet, but I have it on good authority that the two of them are working on the matter,' she said with a gratified smile.

'Now I need to ask you about the events just after Mandy Summers found the body.'

'Well, we heard a scream and rushed up the stairs to find Mandy on the landing. Then Jack went into the bedroom, and I took her down to the lounge and gave her a glass of water. Then, I went back upstairs to see if there was anything I could do, but Jack told me he was dead and said I should go and look after Mandy. He was very upset, so I went back to the lounge and stayed with Mandy until George came back down a few minutes later.'

'When you went upstairs the second time, did you go into the bedroom?'

'Very briefly. Jack was kneeling on the floor beside Justin's body, and he was talking to him in a hushed tone. He looked totally devastated, and it was a terribly sad, almost pitiful moment to watch.'

'Do you have any of the players' wives or girlfriends on your books, Mrs Peacock?'

'Yes, quite a few actually. Shall I make a list for you?'

'That would be very helpful. By the way, are any of the ladies here this morning with you?' asked Parrot.

'Yes, Brenda Maguire and Jackie Buckland have been with me for some time, and Linda Tovey has just signed up.'

Parrot looked slightly bemused. 'Linda Tovey is Mick Harmer's fiancé, Sir,' said Sweeney.

'Yes, thank you, Sergeant. Well, that's all, Mrs Peacock. Now, if you and your husband would be good enough to give your statements to one of the officers outside, then after that, you are both free to go,' said Parrot.

After Janice Peacock swept elegantly from the room, Sweeney turned to his boss. 'I think we should question Justin Brett's teammates, Sir.'

'Just what I was thinking, Sergeant. Let's talk to Terry Maguire first. What position does he play, by the way?'

'He's a defender, Sir, old-fashioned center half, big and strong and good in the air. He's improved in the last couple of years and is a regular in the England squad these days, if not in the team; general consensus is that he's a very good club player but not skillful or quick enough to play against top class international opposition. 'Okay, let's get on with it. Wheel him in, then tell Buckland and Harmer that we shall need to talk to them shortly,' Parrot said with a sense of urgency.

A few minutes later, Sweeney returned with Terry Maguire and Parrot's first thoughts were that he was surely looking at a rugby union forward and not a footballer, such was the size of the man standing in front of him and towering over his sergeant, who was himself over six feet tall. Parrot introduced himself then invited him to sit down. 'Now, Mr Maguire, you obviously know Justin Brett has been murdered, so I need you to tell me in detail everything you can remember from the time you arrived here yesterday.'

'We got here around four-thirty with Johnny and Jackie Buckland. There was a good crowd here already. We went into the garden, got some drinks, and met up with Micky and Linda. We got chatting, then Justin put some goalposts on the lawn, and some of the other lads started to have a kick about.'

'Did you join in, Mr Maguire?' asked Sweeney.

'No, I've got a slight groin strain, so I didn't want to aggravate it. The club doctor says it should clear up in a week or so; anyway, the England squad is announced in a fortnight to play two world cup qualifiers, and I wasn't going to risk missing out for the sake of a bit of fun.'

'Did your teammates join in?' asked Parrot.

'Not straight away, but Justin kept badgering them to play, until Micky went in goal, and Johnny went on with a fake smile and said that he was going to stop the poacher scoring, but, of course, that didn't happen. Justin always took his football seriously; he was even wearing his trademark golden boots for a friendly little five a side on his lawn. He got the ball, beat Johnny, and hit a fierce shot past Mickey…and to see him celebrate, you would have thought he'd just scored the winning goal in a Wembley cup final. Well, that was the poacher's last shot, I guess.'

'To your knowledge, did Justin show anybody at the party his golden boot award?'

'He showed everybody, Mr Parrot. He was always flashing them about. He even used to bring them into the dressing room and would place them on a ledge for everyone to see. It was like he wanted to remind everyone that he was top dog. But if you ask me, he was really trying to convince himself.'

'Did you get on well with him?' asked Sweeney.

'Not particularly. We never really hit it off from day one. He was only seventeen, and he swaggered into the club like he owned the place. Basically, he was a selfish show off. He could be good fun, but, most of the time, he was just hard work. His mood would suddenly change, like some people when they've had too much to drink, except he didn't drink. His mood swings were so wild that sometimes I thought he might be bi-polar.'

'How did your other teammates get on with him?' asked Parrot.

'Friendly enough for the most part, especially Micky; they seemed to get on really well; yet, it was almost as if Justin would deliberately go out of his way to antagonize and upset him, then, five minutes later, he wanted to be mates again. Like I said, Mr Parrot, he was hard work.'

'So tell me, Mr Maguire, why did you attend a party hosted by someone that you disliked?' asked Parrot.

'It wasn't my decision, Mr Parrot,' Maguire said with a smile. 'I came along because Jackie and Brenda wanted to come down here, and I'm sure Johnny Buckland will tell you the same.'

'Were there any other of your teammates here yesterday?' asked Sweeney.

'Yes, a couple of the younger lads turned up. Mickey reckoned that they only came so they could impress their girlfriends, and they left fairly early.'

'Was there anybody else here yesterday connected to the club?' asked Parrot.

'Our first team coach, Steve Pritchard, was here for a couple of hours.'

'Steve Pritchard,' said Parrot. 'That name rings a bell.'

'Top class player in his day and a top class bloke,' said Maguire.

'Was he here with his wife?' asked Sweeney.

'No, they split up a few months ago, although he doesn't seem too bothered…if he is, he's hiding it very well,' said Maguire.

'Did you notice what time Justin Brett went to bed?' asked Parrot.

'Yes, as a matter of fact, I did. Well, I should say my wife and Jackie did. It was just after midnight, and Brenda said something like, "What's up with him? Can't be feeling too well."'

'What exactly did she mean by that, do you think?'

'Justin had a playboy reputation, Mr Parrot, and was always the last person to leave a party. Come to think of it, I seem to remember him yawning a bit earlier. Probably hadn't got any sleep the night before.'

'Yes, probably. Well, that's all for the time being, Mr Maguire. Thanks for your help.'

'That's another suspect up on the blackboard, Sir,' said Sweeney. 'Although, he was very open about his feelings towards Justin Brett.'

'I imagine his feelings were fairly common knowledge, Sergeant. Nothing to gain by hiding them,' Parrot said pragmatically.

'Shall I ask Johnny Buckland to come in, Sir?'

'No, let's have Jackie Buckland and Brenda Maguire in together. Let's hope they compete with each other to dish the dirt.'

Sweeney returned with the two women a few minutes later and made the introductions; then, they sat down close to each other on the sofa, like the best friends they were.

'Right, ladies, you are both obviously aware of why Sergeant Sweeney and I are here. Right now, I have to tell you that we have very little concrete evidence.

So I am relying on the two of you to provide us with as much background information as you possibly can. No matter how trivial it may seem, it could be crucial to solving Justin Brett's murder.'

Sweeney couldn't help breaking into a slight smile. *Sly old fox,* he thought. *Make their gossip appear important and then hope they perform a loose-lipped double act.*

'What sort of thing are you interested in, Chief Inspector?' said Brenda.

'Well, obviously, if you know of any reason why someone would want to harm Justin and perhaps you may be able to give us an insight into his private life, which could be important for us to establish a motive for his murder,' Parrot said in a solemn voice.

'Well, Chief Inspector,' said Jackie, 'there are plenty of people he's upset since he's been at the club.'

The comment received a compliant nod from Brenda, who then said, 'That's right, Mandy Summers for one.'

'How did he upset Ms Summers?' Parrot enquired.

'He dumped her about six weeks ago,' said Brenda. 'That wiped the smile off the snooty bitch's face I can tell you,' she continued.

'Too right,' echoed Jackie. 'Showing off her goods for the entire world to see, then prancing around like Lady Muck. We split a bottle of Chablis when we heard, didn't we, Bren?' she said with a high-pitched laugh.

'Do you know why he broke off their relationship?' asked Sweeney.

'Well, we didn't at the time, but a little bird told us about a week ago that it was because he'd started seeing Lily Peacock on the sly,' said Jackie.

'Is Jack Peacock aware of their relationship?' asked Parrot.

'Old Jack,' said Brenda, shaking her head slowly. 'No, I wouldn't have thought so; the only thing he's aware of is his commission checks. He didn't even know that his own son was gay until Jack junior brought his boyfriend home for the weekend a couple of years ago.'

'Do you think Janice Peacock knows?'

'I would think so. There's not much that escapes that one,' said Jackie.

'Now, what else can you tell us about Justin Brett?' asked Parrot.

The two women looked at each other and exchanged girly laughs. Then Brenda said, 'If Justin had been born a girl, Mr Parrot, he would have been a prize slag. He tried it on with just about every wife and girlfriend at the club and succeeded with a lot of them.'

'Neither of you two ladies succumbed to his charms, then?' said Sweeney.

'No, we didn't,' Jackie said, but not too indignantly. 'But, he never gave up trying, though; he took absolutely no notice of constant refusals. Just seemed to make him keener, even propositioned us together once, didn't he, Bren?'

'He did, the cheeky buggar, wanted both of us in the visitors changing room and wearing the teams away strip, would you believe, Mr Parrot?'

'Can you tell me the names of the women he had relationships with, and I mean the ones that you both can be definite about?' Parrot said.

The two women once more exchanged looks, before Jackie Buckland said, 'I know I speak for Brenda when I tell you that we are uncomfortable doing this.'

Sweeney thought, *Right, you're about as uncomfortable as a cat curled up on a blanket for the night with a passive mouse for company.*

Parrot looked with some sympathy at the two women, although he possessed very little and said, 'If we can positively establish his liaisons, then it may provide a possible motive either by the person involved or by their partners who could have discovered the associations, so it is vital you tell us. Remember, you are helping a murder investigation, not spreading gossip.'

'Well, there was Linda Tovey for sure,' said Brenda. 'We saw them together, coming out of his apartment one Saturday morning. Later, when we tried to warn her off, she said that she just wanted to see what all the fuss was about and that he wasn't all that he was cracked up to be and that he was more interested in doing push-ups on the carpet than he was doing them on her.'

'Is it possible that Mick Harmer could have found out?'

'Not a chance,' said Jackie. 'This happened before they got engaged. I can't see any man going through with an engagement after finding his girlfriend had slept with his supposed best friend.'

'Did either of you notice any friction between them yesterday?' asked Sweeney.

'No. They were very lovey-dovey, weren't they, Bren?' Jackie said.

'Very,' said Brenda, then added, 'That Linda's a cool one, butter wouldn't melt.'

'Was he involved with anyone recently?' Parrot asked.

'He had a fling with Maggie Pritchard a few months ago,' Jackie said.

'That would be Steve Pritchard's wife?' enquired Sweeney.

'Correct,' said Brenda. 'Steve found out and left her.'

'Doesn't that make Mr Pritchard's job difficult?' asked Sweeney.

'Well, I would have thought so, too, but my Terry reckoned they still got on very well. Maybe Steve thought Justin did him a favor.'

'To your knowledge, ladies, was there anybody else here yesterday that Justin had been involved with, or maybe someone who had a partner and split up, because of an affair with Justin Brett?'

Both women shook their heads, and Brenda said, 'No, Chief Inspector. When he dumped them, they stayed dumped, all apart from Mandy Summers; she's been hanging around him like a bad smell.'

'Just one last question, ladies. Mr Maguire mentioned that you both noticed Justin going up to bed quite early last night,' said Parrot.

'On his own, Mr Parrot, very unusual,' Jackie said, laughing. 'Bren and I said he must have been shagged out from the night before,' then she added, 'literally,' at which they both began to cackle.

'Just one last question. After Justin had gone to bed, do you remember where the remaining guests were?'

'Oh that's easy, Mr Parrot,' said Jackie, 'We all went outside to the patio around the pool area.'

'Was anybody still inside the house, or do you re-member anyone going back into the house?'

'I'm pretty sure we were all outside; then, I guess we all went inside at some stage or another to use the bathroom.'

'Did you notice if anyone was missing for a longer period?'

'Not really,' said Brenda, 'but I can tell you that Jackie and I paid our visits together.'

'Well, thank you very much, ladies. That's all for now; you've been a great help,' Parrot said, with a certain amount of relief.

After they left, Sweeney said, 'Well, Sir, those two certainly do their best to live up to their stereotype.'

'True, Sergeant, but very useful stereotypes if what they told us is true. For instance, why didn't Mandy Summers tell us that she'd been dumped?'

'Well, we've only got the word of those two, Sir, and they plainly can't stand her; plus, she did tell us that they hadn't been involved physically for some time.'

'Point taken, Sergeant. Let's have Ms Tovey in now.'

Sweeney returned a few minutes later with Linda Tovey, who Parrot and Sweeney thought was a very attractive young lady with a smile that lit up the room. Parrot went straight for the jugular and said, 'It's been suggested that you had an affair with Justin Brett, is that true?'

'I can guess who by, Chief Inspector; I saw the pantomime dames leave this room a few minutes ago,' to which George Parrot and Daniel Sweeney both had to use their utmost control not to burst out laughing at a very well-founded observation.

'Would you please confirm or deny the allegation, Ms Tovey?'

'I deny it, of course. Justin tried it on once, but I told him that I loved Mick and that I didn't think he should be propositioning someone who was going out with his best mate. I told him that he had no honor, and he got really upset and apologized; then, he begged me not to tell Mick.'

'And did you?' asked Sweeney.

'No, it would have served no purpose,' she answered firmly.

'Ms Tovey, I have to tell you that you were seen leaving Justin Brett's apartment building with him one Saturday morning. Is that true? And if so, would you please explain the reason?'

'It was early afternoon actually, Chief Inspector, and I'd gone round there late morning to talk to Justin.'

'Can you tell us the purpose of your visit?'

'Certainly, for the previous week or so he had constantly subjected Mick to all sorts of ridicule and sarcasm in front of other people. Mick was upset and didn't understand why he was being so callously singled out. So, I thought it might have something to do with me. So, I asked him, and he laughed, then apologized, and said something very strange.'

'What exactly did he say, Ms Tovey?'

'He said that I was barking up the wrong tree and that he knew he was in the wrong, but, sometimes, he couldn't help himself. Then, he promised to engage brain in the future, apologized again, and we left together and went our separate ways.'

'Why then did you tell Brenda Maguire and Jackie Buckland that you were disappointed with Justin's sexual performance when they tried to warn you off, they say, with good intentions?' probed Parrot.

'Purely for their benefit, Chief Inspector, and I doubt very much if either of those two know the meaning of good intentions. They may act like sisters, but they are strictly the ugly variety, I'm afraid, but I thanked them anyway, mainly because I didn't want Mick to know about my visit, innocent though it was and one really with good intentions.'

'Have you had any idea since what he meant by barking up the wrong tree?'

'Not a clue, I'm afraid, but at least my visit wasn't in vain. Justin was sweetness and light to Mick after that.'

'Did you notice anything out of the ordinary about Justin last night?' asked Parrot.

'Not particularly. He said he was excited about playing in his first world cup next year and that he needed to get away for a break after the qualifiers in a couple of weeks. Asked Mick and I if we fancied making up a foursome. I must admit to being intrigued by who the fourth person was, but, when Mick asked him, he tapped the side of his nose with his finger and said, "Wait and see." The only other thing was that he said he felt tired, which was unusual for Justin. He kept yawning and went to bed very early, for him anyway.'

'It was also suggested earlier that he was tired because of a lack of sleep the night before. Any comments about that, Ms Tovey?'

'None whatsoever, Chief Inspector. I really don't enjoy gossiping about other people. To me, it says that the people who need to resort to that sort of thing have very boring lives.'

Parrot wanted to say 'Quite right' and 'well said,' but he resisted the urge, and, instead, thanked her for her candor and told her that she could go. Parrot then turned to Sweeney. 'There's something not quite right, Sergeant. It's not exactly staring us in the face, but I'm convinced there's something, some important fact about this case we've yet to uncover.'

There was nothing for Sweeney to add, but he had heard his boss make similar statements before and invariably been proved correct. 'So, who's next, Sir, Johnny Buckland or Mick Harmer?' asked Sweeney.

'Let's have Mr Harmer in, Sergeant. I'm anxious to hear why his supposed best friend treated him so shabbily.'

Sweeney duly brought in Mick Harmer, and Parrot wasted no time in posing the question uppermost in his mind, to which the young goalkeeper replied, 'I really don't know, Mr Parrot, believe me. I thought long and hard trying to fathom Justin out, but he was a very complicated guy with so many different personalities that I gave up trying in the end.'

'So you decided to tolerate your friend's sudden change of moods?'

'It was better that way and saved a lot of hassle. I'm an easy going sort of bloke, but I would be lying if I said that he never got to me.'

'And when he did get to you, how did you react?'

'I would make a joke out of it sometimes, which I knew infuriated him, or I would just walk away, knowing he would come after me to apologize. Justin was the expert on apologies, Chief Inspector.'

'How did he seem to you yesterday? Was he moody?'

'No. For the last couple of weeks he's been very good natured.'

'Any idea why that might have been?'

'It could be that he had a new mystery girlfriend.'

'Strange he didn't tell you her name,' said Parrot.

'Not really. He could be very secretive or he would tell me intimate details, knowing that I had no interest, but that was exactly the reason he told me. Justin was a man of opposites who delighted in confounding and shocking people.'

'What kind of things was he secretive about?'

'Well, thinking back, sometimes he would disappear for a few days, and, if anyone asked him however innocently where he had been or did he enjoy himself, he would explode, saying mind your own f—ing business.'

'Did he ever explode at you?'

'Just the one time. I learned that day not to ask him those types of questions in the future.'

'When did you sign for the club, Mr Harmer?' asked Sweeney.

'Just over four years ago, as reserve goalie. Then, I became the regular first choice goalkeeper about two and a half years ago.'

'And you are now in the England squad is that correct?'

'Yeah, I've started in a couple of matches, and I've come on as a substitute six times.'

'Justin must have been pleased to have his best mate with him on England duty.'

'You would think so, but opposites again, sergeant. When I got my first call up, the player who normally shared with Justin, knowing that we were good friends, offered to find another roommate. Justin then accused him of being disloyal and saying that he saw enough of me as it was. So there you have a snapshot of a very unpredictable guy who I sadly concluded some time ago was a deeply disturbed and troubled soul.'

'When you first came to the club, was Justin friendly towards you?' asked Parrot.

'No. He hardly said a word to me for the first year, and I only got to know him when I became a regular in the first team.'

'How did he get on with the rest of the team?'

'He didn't. You can tell that by the fact that there were only three of us here yesterday, and two of them came under sufferance.'

'Did he get on with your fiancé?'

'He told me that he liked her and thought we were good together. So when we got engaged, I asked him to be my best man, and he turned me down. His excuse was that he wasn't good at speaking in public and would be too nervous. I said that he only had to toast a couple of bridesmaids, but he wouldn't budge. But, I guarantee that if I had asked someone else he would have erupted.'

'Going back to the time you became friends; did you spend much time together?'

'Sure, he showed me a whole new world. Fancy clubs, restaurants, and some incredibly seedy places, which he got a big buzz from. We used to double date a lot, but, inevitably, Justin would get fed up with his partner, become obnoxious, and the girls had no option but to leave. I've lost count of the number of times that happened. Then, once or twice, when we were on our own after they had left, he would get very serious and talk to me about some pretty weird stuff.'

'Please go on, Mr Harmer. What kind of stuff?' asked Parrot.

'He would talk about his family, especially his mother. He told me he used to lay awake at nights imagining she was dead. He absolutely detested her, and he hated his dad for not protecting him when he was young.'

'Did he actually tell you that she physically assaulted him when he was a child?' asked Parrot.

'No. I got the impression it was more mental and verbal abuse. The way he told me was scary, Chief Inspector. His eyes would glaze over, and he would stare straight ahead as he was telling me these traumatic stories of his childhood. I don't know how much of it was true and how much he had imagined. I've met his family, and they all seemed perfectly normal. His behavior made me feel very uncomfortable, so much so that I would look away, not that Justin noticed; he was somewhere else. It seemed as if he was in some sort of self-induced trance, and then he would speak very deliberately and in a slightly different voice than his usual one. When it first happened, I thought he was just larking around, but it didn't take me long to realize that it was no joke, Chief Inspector.'

'How many times did this happen? And what did he talk about?'

'Only a couple of times, and he would largely be talking about himself, things like, poor little Justin, nobody wants me, nobody loves me, and Mummy hates me. Then, suddenly, his face would break into a sort of dreamy smile, and he would say, "but I don't care, Jackson loves me, and I love Jackson, and we're going away together"; it was all very harrowing; yet, two minutes later, he would be laughing and joking as though he hadn't a care in the world.'

'It sounds like he had regressed back to childhood, Sir, and was talking about an imaginary friend,' ventured Sweeney.

'Just what I was thinking, Sergeant. Did you ever mention Jackson to him, Mr Harmer?'

'Yes, he told me that Jackson was his brother, and when I said that I thought his brother's name was Robert, he said that Jackson Brett was his dead twin brother. I didn't pursue the conversation, Mr Parrot.'

'Do you know if he ever had psychiatric counseling?'

'If he did, he never talked about it with me. Knowing Justin, he wouldn't discuss any subject if he thought it made him appear weak or damaged.'

'So let me ask you, Mr Harmer,' said Parrot, in a bothersome manner, 'why on earth did you remain friends with Justin Brett, a person who, by your own admission, consistently treated you with, if I may say so, contempt?'

'You know, Chief Inspector, I've lost count of the number of people who have asked me that question, and lord knows I've asked it of myself often enough.

The simple truth is that I genuinely liked his company because he could be great fun, but I suppose more than anything, I saw through the bravado and recognized his vulnerability, and that made me feel sad for him and so thankful for my parents, who I love dearly and gave me all the things that Justin never experienced. My father used to say to me that you have to accept the whole package with friends, warts and all, and Justin certainly had his fair share of warts.'

'Did he ever discuss Mandy Summers with you?'

'He told me that he loved her. He said that she was the only woman he'd ever met who he really felt truly comfortable with. So what does the idiot do? He very deliberately sets out to push her away.'

'How exactly did he do that?' asked Sweeney.

'He started to go out with other girls and took them to places where he knew the press would be waiting. Four or five days later of seeing her boyfriend on the front page of every tabloid newspaper kissing and cuddling different women and Mandy told him where he could go.'

'Why didn't he just break it off?'

'Oh no, not Justin…that would have been far too easy,' said Harmer sarcastically. 'He would have had to actually talk to her one to one, and he couldn't handle that.'

'You said that you met Justin's family, and they appeared perfectly normal. When and where was that, Mr Harmer?' asked Parrot

'It was at Frank Peacock's place about two years ago.'

'Did you speak to his mother?'

'Only briefly. Like I said, she seemed normal.'

'Can you recall what she was like physically and if Justin resembled her?' asked Parrot.

'She was tall, slim, and good looking, just like Justin.'

'Did you meet Justin's dad?'

'I'd met Mr Brett, or Kenny, as he likes to be called, quite a few times before in the club bar after a match; sometimes, he would come on the coach with us to local away games.'

'What was your impression of him, and did Justin look like him?'

'Everybody likes Kenny. He's unassuming and just a really nice, regular bloke. There is or was a resemblance between them, but I would say that Justin probably favored his mothers side of the family more.'

'Have you met his brother and sister?'

'Robert and Alison, oh yeah, many times. They both really take after Kenny in personality as well as looks.'

'Have you met Johnny, Kenny's brother?'

'A few times, once at Frank Peacock's house and a couple of times at the club. Very similar to Kenny: easy-going, down-to-earth type of bloke has a reputation as a bit of a ladies' man.'

'One last question. After Justin went to bed, what did you do?'

'Everyone sat outside around the pool area for the next couple of hours; then, we went to bed about two-thirty.'

'Right, Mr Harmer, that's all for now. Thanks for your help,' said Parrot.

Sweeney turned to his boss as Mick Harmer left the room and said, 'Sounds like Justin Brett had more than a few loose screws, Sir.'

'He sounds a very sad case to me. Terry Maguire thought he might be bi-polar; from what I've heard, I'd say he was positively schizophrenic. I'll leave you to interview Mr Buckland. I want a quick word with Jack Peacock before he leaves, and we need to speak to Steve Pritchard so dig out his address, please, Sergeant.'

Parrot caught up with the Peacocks and shepherded Jack Peacock to the rear of the Lodge for a private word.

'Just a couple of issues that have arisen that you may be able to help with, Mr Peacock.'

'Of course, Mr Parrot, you fire away,' he said helpfully.

'Did Justin Brett have a twin brother who died at birth?'

'Yes, he did, but the poor little blighter died when he was four months old.'

'What was the cause of death?'

'They couldn't find anything medically wrong with the little kiddie; put it down to cot death.'

'What was the baby's name?'

'They called him Jackson, after Johnny and Kenny's grandfather.'

'Were they identical twins, Mr Peacock?'

'Two peas in a pod, you couldn't tell which was which. Kenny even had their names put on their baby clothes so he could tell them apart.'

'Twins seem to run in the two families, Mr Peacock?' said Parrot.

'Have done for generations. I've got twin uncles, and Johnny and Kenny have a twin aunt and uncle, but Justin and Jackson were the first identical twins since Grandfather Jackson and his brother Simeon. Rumor has it that my old grandma and Simeon had a fling, which produced my uncles, Mr Parrot, but who knows… lost in the mist of time as they say.'

'Are Robert and Alison Brett twins as well?'

'No, Alison's about two years younger than her brother.'

'By the way, Mr Peacock, what is the Christian name of Justin's mother?'

'Her name is Melinda, Chief Inspector, Melinda Annabella Brett.'

'Well, thanks again, Mr Peacock. We'll be in touch,' said Parrot before heading back to see if Dr. Harry Starkey had any news for him.

'Not much more I can tell you at the moment, George. We'll be taking the body back shortly for the autopsy. I'll call you later if anything interesting turns up.'

'Thanks, Harry. I'll be on my mobile after seven thirty.'

'Taking Audrey somewhere nice?'

'Sarah and Mark are taking us to the Crooked Chimney.'

'Well, in that case, I won't call you,' said the doctor, smiling.

'That's okay, Harry. I'm sure we're both used to interruptions.'

'I'll interrupt you in person then. I'm taking Sheila there tonight for her birthday. The curtailed shopping expedition earlier was to find her a suitable outfit for this evening.'

'Look, I don't want to spoil your romantic plans, Harry, but why not make it a table for six? Sarah would love to see you and Sheila; you are her Godparents after all.'

'Put like that, how can we refuse? I'll get Sheila to change the reservation.'

'Right, see you later. I'm off to see if my trusty sergeant has found Justin Brett's killer.'

Parrot returned to the study to find Sweeney still interviewing Johnny Buckland. His sergeant paused to introduce his boss and then said, 'I'm just about through here, Sir, unless you have any questions.'

'No, I don't think we need to detain Mr Buckland any further, Sweeney,' said Parrot, who was eager to compare notes with his sergeant.

After Johnny had left, Parrot asked, 'Anything of interest from our Mr Buckland?'

'Not really, Sir. The same answers as Terry Maguire. He didn't particularly like Justin Brett, although I would say less intensely than his teammate and he did say they were going to miss his goals. He reckons the club might struggle next season without them.'

'There's a sorry epitaph, Sergeant, being missed for your goals. Did you locate Mr Pritchard's address by the way?'

'Spider, I mean Constable Webb, is getting it, Sir. Apparently, it's not that far, according to Johnny Buckland. He said he spoke to him yesterday at the party, and Pritchard said it was only a twenty-minute drive from here.'

'Good. Give Pritchard a call to let him know we are on our way to question him. After that, Sergeant Sweeney, you can have the undoubted pleasure of taking me back home.'

As the two policemen were driving to Pritchard's house, Sweeney said to his boss, 'I've been thinking, Sir, do you think it would be worthwhile asking a professional profiler to evaluate Justin Brett for us?'

'Profile of the victim…that's different, Sergeant, and it makes excellent sense. Well done; I'll leave it to you to arrange, but I would recommend that you contact Professor Agnes Maxim at the university. She's been a great help to us in the past.'

'I'll call her first thing on Monday morning, Sir.'

'Don't let a good idea wait, Sergeant. Call her as soon as soon as we arrive at Pritchard's place.'

'But she won't be at the university today, will she?'

'There's a good chance she's there; if not, the station has her home and mobile numbers.

'Won't she mind being disturbed, Sir?'

'No. On the contrary, she lives only for her work. I guarantee your call will be received warmly, and she will probably call you "Dear Boy" quite a lot. She may appear a bit dotty, but don't be fooled; she's as sharp as a razor is our Dame Agnes.'

'What do I call her, Sir?'

'Professor, and when you get to know her a bit better, Dame Agnes, although she is the least formal person I've ever met.'

As instructed, Sweeney made the phone call the minute they arrived. Parrot went on ahead and rang the doorbell of the quintessential English cottage, complete with an informal array of ornamental and edible plants in the densely planted front garden. The door opened, and a large, fit-looking man, dressed casually in jeans and an England football shirt, held out his hand and said, 'Steve Pritchard, pleased to meet you, Mr Parrot. Is Sergeant Sweeney not with you?'

'He will be in shortly, Mr Pritchard. In the meantime, I just have a few questions for you, the first being what time did you arrive at Justin Brett's place yesterday and when did you leave?'

'I got there around eight-thirty and left just before midnight.'

'Did you come straight home?'

'Yes, I did, watched a bit of news, then went to bed about twelve forty-five.'

'Did you talk to Justin Brett yesterday?'

'Hardly at all. We had a brief chat in the kitchen about the team's chances next season, and that was about it.'

'How was his mood? Did he seem in good spirits?'

'I would say he was in an exceptionally good mood.'

'You live here on your own, Mr Pritchard?'

'My wife and I split up two months ago, and I moved here shortly after.'

'What made you choose this place?'

'Peace and quiet, Chief Inspector, and a place to think things out.'

'Is there any truth in the rumor that the reason you and your wife have separated is that she was having an affair with Justin Brett?'

'I don't know where you heard that rubbish, but it's totally untrue…believe me.'

'So, if that was not the reason for your break up, would you mind telling what was?'

'No, I don't mind and to tell the truth, I've been racking my brain to come up with the answers, but, in the end, I suppose I have to put it down to just two people who have drifted apart. We haven't really been a real couple for some years, but you hope things get better, and, of course, they rarely do.'

'Are there any children?' asked Parrot.

'We have two: David, who will be eighteen next month, and Annie, who is two years younger.'

'How are they coping?'

'Pretty well, considering the upheaval. I don't know how couples deal with separation and divorce when there are young children involved; at least when they're older, you can talk to them more or less as adults.'

'So there is no other woman involved in the break up, Mr Pritchard?'

'No, Chief Inspector, categorically not.'

'Can you think of anyone who hated Justin enough to kill him?'

'Quite a few of the lads at the club disliked him, but nowhere near enough to do him any real harm.'

'I take it you will be staying on here for the time being, Mr Pritchard?'

'Yes, I've signed a six-month lease.'

'Isn't this place a bit out of the way for your job?'

'Not really. The club's training ground is only half an hour by car and I can get to our stadium in less than an hour.'

'Well, I'll leave you in peace Mr Pritchard, thanks for your help,' and with that Parrot returned to the car to find Sweeney engaged in conversation with Professor Maxim.

'Hold on, Professor, Mr Parrot's returned, I'll pass you over,' said Sweeney.

'Hello, Agnes, I'm hoping you can help us on this one.'

'Hello, Georgie,' came the reply. 'Your sergeant has given me the lowdown on this Brett chappie, and, off the top of my head, I'd say he was a paranoid schizophrenic. The boy's childhood is all important; many children create a fantasy world of their own, where they can withdraw into at times of great unhappiness. In his case, the imaginary friend happened to be his identical twin brother and I don't have to tell you how strong that connection can be. The mood swings are quite normal for someone with his condition, and there is a constant battle going on between attraction and rejection, as evidenced in the way he treated his friend Harmer and Mandy Summers. He probably had a deep-seated irrational fear about who knows what, but I'll have a good think about that and get back to you when I can give you some feasible scenarios, okay, Georgie?'

'Thanks, Agnes. Appreciate it as always…be in touch; bye for now.'

'She sounds a right character, Sir.'

'She's a mould breaker without any doubt. Now, Sergeant, tomorrow morning, I want you to take a drive and interview Mrs Pritchard and try to get to the bottom of the break up with her husband. He just told me that there was nobody else involved; see if she says the same.'

'Do you think it's relevant, Sir?'

'To be perfectly honest, I'm not sure, but, without an obvious motive, we need to explore every avenue.'

When Parrot returned home, he was welcomed by his wife, with the words, 'Now, George, I've spoken to Sheila, and we've agreed that there is to be no shop talk between you and Harry tonight.'

'Of course not, dear,' said Parrot unconvincingly. 'We're going out with family and friends for a pleasant evening.'

The Parrots arrived by taxi at the restaurant and found Harry and Sheila Starkey in the bar with Sarah and Mark. The doctor immediately looked at Parrot and said, 'Look everyone, I know we said no case talk tonight, but I need to speak to George for two minutes.' Before he had finished speaking, he was already shepherding his friend outside.

'Just thought I'd tell you before we sat down, George, that I'm certain as I can be that Justin Brett was in a deep sleep when he was attacked. My best guess is that someone put a substance in his drink. We'll know for sure when we get the tox report back.'

'I was thinking along the same lines,' said Parrot. 'Right, thanks, Harry. We had better get back before the ladies read us the riot act.'

The two men re-entered the bar area, and Parrot said with hands half raised, 'Sorry about that, but it was important, and we promise no more shop talk for the rest of the evening.'

'I saw him play for England at Wembley in a friendly against Holland only a few months ago. Scored the winning goal that night; he's not going to be easy to replace,' said Mark.

'I saw that game live on TV,' said Harry. 'He turned the Dutch center back every which way, and then hit a screamer of a shot into the top left hand corner...the crowd went potty.'

'Alright, we give in,' said Audrey. 'So let's make a pact. You three can discuss football as much as you like here in the bar, but when we go into the dining room, not a peep, okay?'

'Okay,' the three men said in unison and immediately went into a small huddle as men in bars tend to do and began to earnestly debate England's national sport.

True to their word, George, Harry, and Mark, did not mention football once they were seated at their table. Mark did pass a comment halfway through the evening about the England rugby team, but his assessment of their forward play tailed off to no more than a whisper, as he was suddenly confronted by three stony female glares. Harry did jokingly complain that, while the male parties were forbidden to discuss football, elsewhere at the table, there was no apparent embargo on TV soaps and talk shows. To which Sheila replied that they were interesting topics, unlike football. The evening flew by, and, as usual, the Parrot party was the last to leave, prompted by the staff laying the tables for the following day's lunch. George and Audrey shared a taxi with the Starkeys and they all agreed that they didn't see enough of each other and promised not to leave it so long until they next got together.

Once inside, Audrey said, 'You look tired, George. Why don't you go up to bed?'

'Yes, I think I will. Early start tomorrow. Are you coming up?'

'Not just yet; there's a late night film I want to watch.'

'Which one?'

'Oh, nothing you would be interested in. It's an old weepy with Rock Hudson and Jane Wyman; you must know the one. It's where they don't get on, then she goes blind, and he becomes an eye surgeon and saves her life at the end.'

'Oh, yes, I remember,' said Parrot, kissing his wife. 'A very funny movie, laughed all the way through it, goodnight, dear.'

Early the following morning, Parrot leapt out of bed, showered, dressed in a flash, and kissed his sleeping wife, with the words, 'You're a treasure.' He then went downstairs, called his sergeant and said, 'Sweeney, after you get back from interviewing Mrs Pritchard, let's meet up and put our heads together.'

'No need, Sir. I spoke to her last night.'

'In person, Sergeant?'

'Yes.'

'Well done, Sweeney. What did she have to say?'

'Quite a lot actually, Sir.'

'Look, where are you now?' interrupted Parrot.

'Just about to leave for the station.'

'Forget that. Come and pick me up. On your way over, think about a place for us to get some breakfast on a Sunday morning.'

Parrot made one phone call while waiting for Sweeney, and, when the conversation ended, he smiled contentedly. Sweeney duly arrived and suggested they try the breakfast at The Truckers Cafe.

'The Truckers Cafe?' repeated Parrot.

'It's either there or one of those plastic Motorway Service Stations, Sir.'

On the way, Sweeney recounted his conversation with Mrs Pritchard or Wendy, as she insisted being called. 'Well, Sir, she was alone and had been drinking, which I'd picked up on when I called her. In fact, it persuaded me to make the journey. I thought she would be more forthcoming, and I wasn't disappointed. She denied having a relationship with Justin Brett but volunteered that she had a few affairs over the years. When I asked her for names, she became, shall we say, very playful, Sir.'

'I hope you didn't play along, Sergeant?'

'Only as far as necessary to get information. Same old story though Sir: husband had neglected her for years, not only sexually but as a person. They hardly spoke anymore and never went out together. She said that, now that the kids were grown up, her life was empty, and she started having affairs for a little bit of attention. Mr Pritchard would often stay at their apartment in town instead of coming home; she was convinced he was seeing other women, which he always denied. She said that she had a brief fling with Johnny Brett a few years ago and with Johnny Buckland more recently.

'Johnny Buckland,' said Parrot. 'Well, that's something his wife and her best friend don't know, eh,' he said with a smile.

'She did mention a couple of other men, but they're not connected to the case. Do you think her statement is significant in any way, Sir?'

'Yes, I do, Sergeant.' Sweeney swung the car into the forefront of the café. 'But, not because of her affairs, and I'll tell you why over breakfast.'

The two policemen, looking like the proverbial fish out of water, ensconced themselves in an unobtrusive end booth after Parrot had ordered two full English breakfasts at the counter on the way in. 'Something has been nagging away at me since yesterday afternoon,' Parrot said. 'Then, it came to me as I woke up this morning, and all because my wife stayed up late last night to watch an old movie.'

'I'm intrigued, Sir, please go on.'

'Well, judging from all the testimony we heard yesterday, I don't think there was any doubt in either of our minds that Justin Brett was a very complex individual, but I believe that his behavior towards certain people, namely Mandy Summers and Mick Harmer, can be explained by a deeply hidden trait in his character that was only known to a very few men.' Parrot paused as two enormous breakfasts were plunked down on the table.

'The suspense is killing me, Sir,' said Sweeney. 'What was this hidden trait?'

'Justin Brett's hidden trait, Sergeant, was that as well as being a ladies' man, he was also attracted to certain men.'

'Yes, of course,' Sweeney said. 'That explains his treatment of Mick Harmer; he must have wanted him.'

'Passionately, I would have thought,' said Parrot. 'And can you imagine his frustration at seeing this man naked in the showers every day and knowing his friend, and I stress friend, was straight and very happy with his fiancé. Remember what he said to Linda Tovey about barking up the wrong tree. It wasn't her that he was interested in at all. Rather her boyfriend. I spoke to Agnes Maxim this morning, and she confirmed my suspicions as being very likely. But, as she explained, Justin wasn't promiscuous; he became physically attracted to certain men only when they had become friends. They were, in essence, adult Jackson Bretts. He felt so comfortable with Mick Harmer, that he even allowed him to hear his innermost thoughts. Then, having done so, he would treat him badly, because in reality, Mick Harmer could never be a total substitute. Agnes also said that his sudden disappearances for days at a time were probably spent in a retreat somewhere with a male companion. She pointed out to me how difficult life must have been for him as a footballer, a profession with a never-ending barrage of testosterone filled jokes, asides, and innuendos, which I'm sure he laughed along with, for his own sad, self-loathing protection.

'So all the bravado and the womanizing was just an act?' asked Sweeney.

'No, not at all. He genuinely liked women sexually, but Mandy Summers was different. She was the first woman that he actually liked in the whole of his life. They were good friends, he told her personal memories of his childhood that no woman before, I would wager, had been allowed to share. But then panic, as Agnes explained. The sudden realization that this girl that he adored could discover his innermost depravity, as he saw his weakness. This forces him to act appallingly, in a desperate effort to compel her to end the relationship.'

'They remained friends though, Sir,' said Sweeney.

'He still liked Mandy and, now, with the threat of discovery lifted, he could still meet her as a friend. As Agnes explained it to me, Justin's inner turmoil centered around his love for a dead twin brother, who he turned to in an effort to create a world where he was loved, a world far removed from his actual life. So, every time there was a harsh word or look from his mother, he took refuge in his imaginary retreat, which more and more became a very real sanctuary to him in times of unhappiness.'

'So he was in denial, even as a young child?' asked Sweeney.

'Serious denial, Dame Agnes reckons, that became more emotionally difficult for him to handle when he reached puberty and was suddenly confronted with mixed and complicated sexual feelings.'

'Poor Buggar,' said Sweeney. 'Do you think Jack Peacock junior could be involved? Brenda Maguire did let slip that he was gay, and it might explain Justin Brett's disappearing acts. He could have been staying with Jack junior at or near the University.'

'Did Constable Webb give you a list of every one at yesterday's party?'

'Slipped my mind to ask him. sorry, Sir, I'll call him now.'

'I'm mainly interested to see if Lily or Jack junior turned up.

'So, either one of them could have been Justin's new love interest, or that, in turn, was the reason for asking the Peacocks over on Saturday morning, Sir.'

'A valid assumption, Sergeant, and what if the brother or the sister had already told their father of their involvement with Justin. How could he tell them that they were half siblings without risking the whole world finding out about a well-kept, twenty-five-year-old secret? A major dilemma for Jack Peacock with no obvious solution, except a murder maybe.'

'Do you have a main suspect in mind, Sir?'

'I do, Sergeant, but I don't want to jump the gun before checking a few facts. Now let's finish this delicious breakfast that I shall pay for in consideration of your excellent choice of venue.'

Sweeney learned from Constable 'Spider' Webb that Jack and Lily Peacock were both at Justin Brett's party, and Parrot quickly decided to pay the Peacock household a visit. Twenty minutes later, the two policemen were being warmly invited inside by Jack Peacock senior.

'Please make yourselves comfortable gentlemen,' he said, waving his arm at an array of chairs. 'Now, what can I do for you?'

'Are your daughter and son at home, Mr Peacock?'

'No, they went out last night and stayed overnight with their sister. Should be back before lunch, though.'

'Is your wife in the house?'

'Gone to church like she does every Sunday. Never misses, even when we're on holiday abroad. First thing she does is check out the local church.'

'Would I be right in thinking she is a Catholic?'

'Yes, you would, Mr Parrot, a devout Catholic, unlike this old lapsed reprobate who sits before you.'

'Are the Brett family Catholic?'

'Yes, all of them; that's how Johnny Brett and I first met as kids. Believe it or not, we sang in the same choir.'

'And Kenny's wife, Melinda, I take it she is of the Catholic faith as well?'

'Yes, she is a very staunch believer as it happens. What's all this leading to, Mr Parrot?'

'I think you know where—Jack,' said Parrot in a serious tone. 'I believe you had an affair with Melinda Brett that resulted in the birth of twins, one of which, Jackson, died at the age of four months. Melinda believed she was being punished for her sin and consequently treated the remaining twin, Justin, very badly. I imagine she found it difficult to even look at the boy because it reminded her every time of her profound shame and guilt. You were more than happy to look after the boy's interest when he decided to becomes a professional footballer, which must have pleased you immensely, but you saw the boy's torment, his unstable mental state, and all you could do was watch from a distance, unable to comfort your own child for fear of revealing the past. Then, to your dismay, you find that Justin is having a relationship with your daughter, and you are finally trapped in what must have been an unimaginable nightmare, with no way out except one. I should tell you that your DNA is being checked against Justin's, so any denial at this stage would be pointless if not true.'

Jack Peacock had listened impassively to the synopsis and then broke into a broad smile, and said, 'I had you booked as a smart one from the first time I clapped eyes on you, Mr Parrot, and I have to admit that you're spot on with everything you've just said. Spot on in every respect but one. I'm not the father of Justin Brett. Your DNA tests will prove that, but I'll tell you now what I've kept quiet about for twenty-five years; my best mate, Johnny Brett, is Justin's father. He's a smashing bloke, Mr Parrot, but when it comes to the ladies, well, he just can't help himself. When Melinda found out she was pregnant, she was distraught. Being a Catholic, an abortion was out of the question, and Kenny and her were not even married at the time, and she had been saving herself until they were. So, she slept with Kenny and, shortly after, told him she was pregnant. They married on the quick and only Melinda, Johnny, and I knew the truth about those kids until today. That's how I got to be Justin's Godfather. Kenny wanted his brother, but he refused under pressure from Melinda...said he wasn't religious and didn't want to be hypocritical. So, Kenny and Melinda asked me. Even though I'm not particularly religious either, I saw it as a necessary duty, if you understand, Mr Parrot.'

'I do understand, Jack, and I appreciate your candor,' said Parrot.

'Can we keep this between the three of us? Can't see how it has anything to do with the boy's murder, even though it had everything to do with the poor little buggar's life.'

'I think everyone connected with that episode has suffered more than enough, Jack, and I'm sure I speak for Sergeant Sweeney when I say that I have no wish to cause any more grief to those involved.'

'Thanks, Mr Parrot, and you, too, Sergeant; it's much appreciated.

'Was your daughter involved with Justin?' said Parrot, anxious to change the subject.

'Janice did tell me they had been seeing each other.'

'What was your reaction?'

'Not best pleased to begin with. Don't get me wrong. I loved the boy, but he wasn't a very kindhearted person, and I worried that my Lily would get hurt. Then, Janice put my mind at rest. She said that if there was anyone who could straighten him out, it was our girl, and she was right, though we'll never see now, will we, Mr Parrot, shame, bloody shame,' Peacock said as tears filled his eyes.

'Do you think that was the reason he invited you over yesterday morning?'

'Probably. Janice reckons it was.'

'What about Lily? Have you spoken to her?'

'Yeah, when we got back yesterday afternoon. She was very upset, so her brother took her to their sister's house for the night. They're all very close, so it made sense. We got a phone call earlier, and they will be back around two o'clock if you want to talk to her.'

'Not today, Jack. We'll come back tomorrow morning around eleven. Thank you again for your help. Come on, Sweeney, we have another call to make.'

As the policemen got into the car and Sweeney said, 'Johnny Brett, eh, that's a turn up. Well, that puts paid to Jack Peacock being your main suspect, Sir.'

'I don't recall mentioning that he was my main suspect, but, for your information, we are now on our way to arrest my main suspect, so let's get going.

'As Sweeney pulled away, he said, 'Are you going to tell me who it is, Sir?'

'Do I have to? You constantly tell me that you intend to take the Inspector's exam, so how about showing me some detecting.'

'Right,' said Sweeney determinedly. 'I would say that by a process of elimination that our man is Steve Pritchard.'

'Can you explain the reasoning behind that conclusion, Sergeant?'

'Well,' said Sweeney, 'Are we heading for Pritchard's place?'

'We are indeed,' said Parrot. 'Now you've given yourself a bit of thinking time, so come on, think motive and opportunity.'

'Right, Sir, his motive was that Justin wrecked his marriage. Opportunity fits. He told you he left the party around midnight. So he could have slipped something into one of those sports drink that Brett liked so much, just before leaving. The timing fits: shortly after Pritchard departs, Justin unusually for him is seen yawning and soon after goes to bed. Pritchard parks his car off the road. Then creeps back unseen into the house. While everyone is outside, he picks up the golden boot that is handily lying around, then goes upstairs to the bedroom, where he knows his intended victim is fast asleep and bludgeons him to death. He then places the boot on a pillow as if to say poetic justice has been done. Or some such rubbish. How am I doing, Sir?'

'Very well, Daniel, but tell me, how exactly did Justin Brett ruin Steve Pritchard's marriage?'

'Well, he had an affair with Wendy Pritch—' said Sweeney, catching himself in mid sentence. Seeing Parrot's knowing smile, he continued, 'No, it was Brett and Pritchard. They were having an affair. He left his wife and moved down here to be close to Justin.'

'Excellent deduction, Sergeant. Sign those papers to take your inspector's exam tomorrow, and that's an order.'

'Yes, Sir. When did you begin to suspect Pritchard?'

'When you related a part of your conversation with Wendy Pritchard.'

'What part exactly, Sir?'

'She told you that her husband preferred to stay in their apartment in town rather than come home. I thought, if that was the case, why walk out of the marital home and move down here when he already has a perfectly good place to stay. No, he moved here because he needed to be near to Justin. The next part is supposition on my part until we question him, but I think that the pair of them, prompted by Brett no doubt, had agreed to live together. Of course, Justin, being an extremely fickle character, meets up with Lily Peacock. They hit it off, and, a few weeks later, he is proposing marriage. So that leaves Pritchard high and dry. A broken marriage and a broken heart. Feeling desperately betrayed, he decides to kill his young friend and lover. He arrives at the party and goes to Justin's bathroom, where he knows the sleeping tablets are kept. He empties the contents into a phial he has brought for that purpose and waits until just before he is about to leave and slips the powder into Justin's drink. I also believe that Pritchard's apartment in town is where Justin could have been found on those occasions he went missing. You heard what Terry Maguire said about Pritchard being a top class bloke, and I'm sure Justin Brett as a raw seventeen-year-old looked up to and later confided his life and its secrets to the good bloke Steve Pritchard undoubtedly is.'

'It's hard to imagine anybody being able to live that kind of life, Sir. I mean, to wake up every morning knowing your day is going to be filled with repression, deceit, and guilt. How do people cope with those feelings?'

'They cope, I suppose, by sharing and enjoying the times when they are able to be totally free of the shackles of those hidden yearnings. As in this case, when Justin and Steve's secret rendezvous allowed them, and I think Steve Pritchard in particular, to behave without those awful destructive feelings. One thing's for sure: the love that dare not speak its name is still alive and kicking in some quarters of modern day life.'

They arrived at Steve Pritchard's cottage, and Sweeney asked, 'Do we have enough evidence to arrest him, Sir?'

'Good point, Daniel, and the short answer is no, but I'm confident that when we confront him with our version of the murder, he will confess.'

Parrot's confident prediction was to prove inaccurate. The two policemen, after getting no reply from the front of the cottage, ventured to the back of the property, where they both peered through a window, to be greeted by the grisly sight of Steve Pritchard hanging from a beam in the dining room. There were two suicide letters, one addressed to his wife and children, begging their forgiveness, and one addressed to Parrot, containing a signed confession to Justin Brett's murder.

Harry Starkey and his team arrived shortly after, and the doctor said, 'What a bloody awful case, George. I saw Pritchard play many times. He was tough as nails on the pitch but after the match, when he was being interviewed, you'd hardly know it was the same person. He was a quietly spoken, shy kind of a fellow, and very likeable. What a tragedy—oh and by the way, the tox report shows substantial amounts of barbiturates in Justin Brett's system. Also, his DNA and Jack Peacock's proved negative.'

'Thanks, Harry, much appreciated, catch up with you later.'

'Where are we going, Sir?' asked Sweeney.

'To see Wendy Pritchard. I don't want her, or her kids to hear the news on the television or radio.'

As Sweeney drove, he said, 'Just a couple of points that puzzle me, Sir.'

'Just a couple from this case, Sergeant...I'd say you were doing very well. Go on. What are they?'

'Why do you think Justin Brett asked Mandy Summers over on Saturday morning? Was he trying to upset her by announcing his engagement to Lily Peacock?'

'No I don't think so; they were genuine friends and he had precious few of those and I honestly believe she would have been very happy for him. She's a quality lady.'

'Yes, she certainly is, Sir. You mentioned earlier that Mrs Parrot watched an old movie last night and that it helped you solve the case.'

'The film that she watched starred Rock Hudson, who in private life was gay. Of course, in those times, the big film studios controlled every aspect of their stars' lives. They even arranged a bogus marriage for him. They couldn't afford to let the public know that their handsome, rugged, leading man was a homosexual. He was a big star, and it would have led to a catastrophe at the box office. So, it struck me suddenly about the similar circumstances in this case, where a very talented young sportsman in the public eye could be harboring a similar secret. Of course, we knew that Justin also liked women, but, once I'd made the possible connection, it was only a short distance to link Steve Pritchard as the likely killer.'

'After we've spoken to Wendy Pritchard, do you fancy a pint at the Feathers, Sir?'

'I do indeed, Daniel, my treat. If you have no plans afterwards, why don't you come back for a Sunday roast?'

'I'd like that very much, Sir, if you're sure Mrs Parrot won't mind.'

'Not at all. She'll be delighted. I'll call and tell her to expect three for lunch.'

The Director's Final Cut

Detective Sergeant Dan Sweeney's unusually early arrival at Hadleigh police station on a particularly cold and windy spring Monday morning had little to do with a heavy workload and everything to do with the return of his boss, Chief Detective Inspector George Parrot, from his annual two-week vacation.

Police Constable Malcolm Webb watched with more than a little amusement as Sweeney took off his saturated raincoat and huffed and puffed and cursed under his breath.

'Something you find funny, Spider?'

'Yes, Sarge, once a year you come in here at the crack of dawn. So it can only mean that Polly's back from his holidays.'

'Don't let him catch you calling him that, but you're right; I got a phone call from him last night. Said he wants to be brought up to date…not that there's much to tell, as I told him, but he insisted like he always does. You know, it's weird; I swear that the two quietest weeks of the year are when he's on vacation; it's as if all the villains decide they don't want to be arrested by anyone else but him and behave themselves for a couple of weeks. I mean, look at the crime statistics since he's been away: a stolen bike with a flat tire, a domestic dispute about the custody of a mangy cat, and an across-the-table punch up at the Barley Mow involving two geriatrics who'd been arguing about the contentious issue of wildlife. Now he's back, and I guarantee there will be a major crime within a week.'

'You're beginning to sound paranoid, Sarge.'

'Having to get out of bed at five thirty on a filthy morning like this gives me the right to be a little paranoid, Spider.'

'I guess so. What time did he say he'd be here?'

'He said about six-thirty, Constable,' came the reply from the doorway, where a suntanned George Parrot stood, directing a wry smile at his two subordinates.

Sweeney returned a smile of sorts and said, 'Good to have you back, Sir. You look very well. Did you and Mrs Parrot enjoy your holiday in Barbados?'

'Yes we did, very much Sergeant. A wonderful place with genuinely, friendly people, plus a crime rate the chief constable would give his right arm for. Would you believe I learned how to scuba dive and Audrey went parasailing?'

'Well, good for you and Mrs Parrot. Shall we go to your office? I'll bring you up to date on what's not been happening.'

'Good idea. Any hot coffee going, Constable? I'm frozen to the marrow. Been used to the early morning sun on my toes for the past couple of weeks.'

'I'll make a fresh pot, Sir, and bring it through to you in a few minutes.'

Sweeney relayed the recent dearth of crime, to which Parrot replied, 'Yes, I heard you expounding your interesting theory to Constable Webb as to the cause of this recent inactivity, though I'm personally reluctant to take total credit for this welcome downturn. So, nothing else of note, Sergeant?'

'Not of a criminal nature, Sir.'

'And of a non-criminal nature?'

'Well, the chief constable called last week. He forgot you were on vacation. He muttered something about being damned inconvenient, and then deigned to leave a message with me for you to act on the minute you returned.'

'And pray tell me what's so important. It must have something to do with the media.'

'Spot on deduction, Sir. It seems that an American film company has leased Hadleigh Hall for three months.'

'Don't tell me he's put me forward for a leading role.'

'Not quite, Sir. He wants you to introduce yourself to the producers and organize a police presence to look after the safety of the stars of the film. Keep the paparazzi at bay, and so forth. He said the national newspapers were bound to arrive in droves, and that it was an excellent opportunity for some high profile PR.'

'This is a job for the uniform division, Sergeant, not a detective inspector. I'll call him later and tell him what I think of his bloody high profile PR.'

'I don't think that will work, Sir. I made the same point, and he dismissed it out of hand. He said that you were his top man; more to the point, you are also well respected by the press.'

'Good Lord, does he think I have nothing more urgent to do than wet nursing a bunch of overpaid, highly strung egotists?'

'I'm afraid that's my fault, Sir. First question he asked me was if we were busy. Thinking he would be pleased, I told him that things were quiet. I'm an idiot, Sir.'

'No you're not, Sergeant. He didn't get to be chief constable without learning how to control people, an art he has perfected and one he performs with considerable relish , so don't blame yourself. He worked his magic on me a few times before I got his measure.'

'Really, Sir? That's a surprise...not that you got his measure; I mean that he managed to pull the wool over your eyes.'

'I've never been political, Sergeant, and I work on the principle of giving people the benefit of the doubt until they prove me wrong. But I dislike the way some people seem to have no qualms about scheming to achieve their aim; and I'm afraid Chief Constable Oswald Rowley falls into that category. Anyway, enough of that. Do you have any gen on these film people?'

'Yes, Sir. I downloaded their biographies; I thought you might want to look at their profiles before meeting them.'

'Good. I'll take a look at them later, but, in the meantime, give me a general breakdown.'

'Well, the film they're making is a historical romance set in England in the 1850s. It's from a bestselling novel by Winifred Creamer, who has also written the screenplay. The director is Charles Jennings, likes to be known as CJ. He is in his early forties, and he's a hot property in Hollywood, won two Oscars in the last five years, and was nominated in another. He's British, started his career making TV commercials, and then made a name for himself as a television director before moving into movies. He moved to Los Angeles twelve years ago. He has a reputation for being ruthless and unkind on set... reduces actors to tears frequently, or so the tabloids say. Been married and divorced three times, and he's currently engaged to Julie Pattison. She's nearly twenty years his junior and the female lead in the film.'

'Is she worthy or are we talking nepotism?'

'No, she was tipped for stardom from a tender age, and all the critics agree that she's a natural and very talented.'

'Is she an American?'

'Born in London...Her mother emigrated to the states when Julie was a young girl.'

'Who's playing the male lead?'

'A virtual newcomer called Jeremy Saville; he's English, mid twenties, and was a soap star in his teens. He's made a few films and received decent reviews.'

'Seems to me they're taking a chance using a comparative novice in what appears to be a big budget film, Sergeant.'

'They must think he's got something. I'm sure these people don't risk their own money lightly. I bet his salary is a fraction of what they would have to pay to an established star.'

'Bit of a heartthrob, is he?'

'Yes, and he has a reputation of being a ladies man.'

'What have you got on the producer?'

'Producers, actually, Sir. Two brothers, John and Oliver Tapley, born in Australia. They made a name for themselves there with low-budget movies that always turned a decent profit. They moved to Los Angeles fifteen years ago and had enormous commercial if not critical success. Then, seven years ago, they won their first Oscar for *The not so White House*, a scathing indictment of American politics about the Nixon years, which won six Academy awards. Three years later, they produced another blockbuster about the American Civil War called *A Country Divided,* which won best film and five Oscars. John Tapley is forty-two, ten years older than his brother, and, by all accounts, very much the senior partner and driving force in their production company. He's been married to the actress Jane Warren for ten years, and they have three children.'

'Does she have a part in the film?'

'No, she gave up a successful career when their first child was born. She is apparently happy being a full time wife and mother, or so she told Oprah on national TV.'

'What about the younger brother?'

'Ran wild as a youngster—booze and broads as they say in the States. His older brother had to bail him out on more than one occasion. It was rumored that he got a fifteen-year-old wannabe into trouble and was facing up to twenty years in jail until a large sum of money was paid to the girl's family…funny enough, the charges were suddenly dropped. Shortly after, he married a fashion model. It lasted a couple of years before they divorced, no children. Since then, he's been man about town and, apart from the odd fracas at his favorite casino, he's straightened himself out.'

'Good work, Sergeant. You've obviously spent a lot of time and energy putting this motley crew together. I suppose we should pay them a visit, but I don't think I can face them until I've had a full English breakfast. I love Barbados, but they've never heard of baked beans, fried bread, or Daddies sauce, not to mention bacon with a rind attached or pork sausages, so let's head for the café, my treat.'

Over breakfast, Sweeney was receiving a lengthy account of the Parrot's Caribbean vacation and was beginning to visibly wilt, when the strains of Hot Chocolate's 'I Believe in Miracles' burst into life on his mobile phone and rescued him.' Excuse me, Sir, better take this; it's the station.

'Parrot waved a compliant hand but was more concerned with mopping up the last remnants of his fry up with a piece of fried bread. Sweeney had a short conversation with 'Spider' Webb and then turned to Parrot and said, 'Looks like my theory could be more than conjecture, Sir; there's been an assault up at the Hadleigh Hall, and you only arrived back on duty three hours ago. Must have smashed your record by a street, Sir.'

'Yes, very droll, Sergeant. Now give me the details before I totally crack up.'

'Sorry Sir. It's Oliver Tapley. He's been taken to hospital with a suspected broken nose.'

'Administered by Mr Charles Jennings no doubt.'

'Absolutely right, but how did you know? I mean, we've not even met them yet.'

'Just an educated guess, sergeant—young, attractive girl, recently engaged to a much older man, and surrounded by a bevy of highly charged testosterone egos, equals jealous fiancé, equals broken nose.'

'Faultless logic, Sir, or an educated guess?'

'Bit of both really...either approach sometimes works. Right. We'd better get up there and speak to this Jennings chap. I did say it was my treat?'

'Yes, you did, Sir, and thanks very much for the delicious tea and toast.'

The weather had improved markedly while the two policemen were indoors enjoying their breakfast, and the sun was breaking through, promising a pleasant spring day. The press assembled in droves as the two policemen arrived at Hadleigh Hall. They immediately surged towards the car.

'Word must have got out about Oliver Tapley, sergeant.'

'This lot probably got wind about it the minute knuckle met bone.'

Cries of, 'They've sent for Polly' and 'Polly's here' and suchlike brought the slightest of smirks to Dan Sweeney's face, but not so slight as to go unnoticed by the ever-astute Parrot.

'Keep driving, sergeant, and get uniform down here to look after our unruly friends from Fleet St.'

'They certainly have a genuine liking for you, Sir.'

'As long as I get results, that will probably continue, but I don't choose to bathe in their unwelcome glory unlike certain senior officers. As far as I'm concerned I'm just doing my job.'

'I understand, but the public needs heroes. It's important that the good guys in the white hats are seen to be winning, and that's what you represent, Sir.'

Sweeney began to smile as he thought of the many headlines about his boss: 'Polly swoops in dawn raid', 'Polly puts blackmailer behind bars', and a picture of him entering his local hostelry, with the caption, 'Polly goes to The Feathers'. Apparently, the chief constable was none too pleased with this particular article. He had called Parrot and said, 'Good God, man, do you have to hand it to the press on a plate? Do you have to drink at a pub with that name? Did you not see the connection? You're my top man...can't afford to have your reputation tarnished.' Parrot had replied that he had been going to 'The Feathers' for fifteen years and that he was off duty, and he certainly couldn't be held responsible for the tabloid's insatiable demand for cheap headlines.

'You're smiling again, Sweeney.'

'Just thinking about all these famous people under one roof. Must be manna from heaven for the chief constable,' he lied.

'Where is the owner of the Hall?'

'I believe he's gone to live in the Caribbean for three months, Sir. It's rumored that the production company paid him half a million dollars to rent the place.'

'Lucky beggar, what about his staff?'

'They're staying on to look after their new tenants.'

Sweeney parked the car amid a host of luxury vehicles and trailers. The two policemen approached a massive wooden entrance door, which was the centerpiece of a rather sinister-looking gothic arch. The door slowly opened to reveal, framed within the setting, a stunning young girl who Sweeney immediately recognized as Julie Pattison. She smiled seductively at Sweeney, who responded with a practiced smile of his own, then said, 'We're here to question Charles Jennings. This is Chief Inspector Parrot, and I'm Sergeant Sweeney.' Both men produced their warrant cards, which Julie Pattison meticulously inspected, lingering that little bit longer over Sweeney's.

'Your photograph doesn't do you justice, Daniel. You're far more handsome in the flesh.'

Sweeney flashed her a smile and replied, 'I can't imagine any photograph that could possibly do you justice.'

An impatient Parrot barked, 'When you're quite ready, Sergeant, we do have an interview to conduct. Where can we find Mr Jennings?'

'He was on the terrace deep in conversation with his film editor a few minutes ago, Chief Inspector. Go down the hallway and into the main lounge, which will lead you to the conservatory. It opens directly on to the terrace, but don't tell him I gave you directions; he's in a foul mood and hates to be interrupted when he's talking, or, should I say, dictating to his crew.'

The two policemen were heading down the hallway when a shrill voice stopped them in their tracks. 'Stop right there.' Parrot and Sweeney turned to find a fierce looking, middle-aged woman marching towards them. She gave them a quizzical look, then said in an authoritative tone, 'Well, why are you wandering around unattended? We are not open to the public for the next three months, and, even if we were, this is a private area.'

Parrot briefly viewed the woman with a certain amount of annoyance, then said, 'We are police officers, madam, and are on our way to the terrace to interview Mr Jennings. And you are?' he asked, fully expecting her to say she was Mrs Danvers, the sinister housekeeper in the Hitchcock thriller 'Rebecca'.

'My name is Victoria Croft, and my brother and I own Hadleigh Hall. Do you have some identification,' came the stern retort. Parrot and Sweeney produced their warrant cards again, which were inspected scrupulously, before Parrot said quietly, 'We're sorry for intruding, but we do need to talk to Mr Jennings, and Ms Pattison pointed us in this direction.'

Victoria Croft's demeanor suddenly changed, and she even managed a faint smile as she said, 'Do forgive me for being so abrupt, Chief Inspector; it's these film people all over the place...I'm just not used to strangers at the Hall. I know they have paid handsomely for the privilege, but I can't help feeling that I've been invaded.'

'Did you not consider holidaying with your brother?'

'Steven did invite me, but I'm not overly keen on the heat, and I would have spoilt his fun. My brother enjoys the nightlife, and I think he might have felt a little uncomfortable with me tagging along. Anyway, it was good of him to offer, but I saw the relief on his face when I declined.'

'Forgive me; is it Ms or Mrs Croft?'

'It's Mrs Croft, Chief Inspector. My husband died some years ago.'

'Do you have any other family living at the Hall?'

'My daughter, Rachael, lives here with me, and so does my brother's youngest son, Jacob, from his first marriage, and my niece, Stephanie, is staying with us for a few months.'

'What's your brother's surname?'

'It's Scarll, Chief Inspector...an unusual name. Its origin is Scandinavian.'

'Are you related to Peter Scarll the composer?'

'Yes, he's our elder brother, Stephanie's father. Are you familiar with his work?'

'A little, but my wife is very fond of his music; she says it's her music to dream by.'

'Yes, she's right. It's gentle and warming, exactly like Peter. He's coming to the hall for the weekend. If you're free, come to lunch on Saturday and bring your wife, Chief Inspector.'

'I couldn't possibly impose; you are overrun already.'

'No, I insist. It'll be very informal. There's a good crowd coming along, and I'm sure your wife would like to meet Peter. Besides, it offers us welcome relief from these film people. Oh, listen to me; I don't mean to sound ungrateful, but a combination of charm and intensity rather gets to me. They take themselves so seriously, you see.'

'Have you spoken to Charles Jennings?'

'Only briefly, for which I'm extremely grateful. Whilst I was welcoming him to the Hall, he was constantly looking around and barking orders to all and sundry. I'm not one for making snap judgments, but I have to say I took an instant dislike to the man, and nothing I've seen and heard since has changed that opinion.'

'What kind of things, Mrs Croft?'

'Well, for one thing, he has a vicious tongue. A few days ago when he was short of extras, he asked Stephanie if she would help and play a walk-on part. She refused because she was too nervous, but he turned on the charm and cajoled her into accepting the part, saying she was very photogenic, which she is, and what a great help she would be to the production. She was asked to play the part of a parlor maid delivering afternoon tea on the terrace, but, when it came to her scene, Jennings erupted at her, saying that she was supposed to be serving tea, not walking down a catwalk pouting like some bloody wannabe model. Stephanie is quiet and rather shy, like her father, and doesn't handle confrontation well. So she ran off in a flood of tears.'

'Did you speak to Jennings?'

'Damn right I did. I told him that he'd paid to be a guest in my house, but that didn't give him the right to be rude to members of my family, and I told him to pack up and that I would return his check less two weeks rent.

'Good for you, Mrs Croft. What did he say to that? I bet the charm offensive went into overdrive,' Parrot said, admiring the woman's spirit.

'He apologized profusely, made some excuse about being behind schedule and overrunning the budget. Although I didn't believe a word. I said that I sympathized, but that he should be apologizing to Stephanie, who, after all, was helping out at his express wish. He said that I was absolutely right, that his behavior was unforgivable, and that he would put things right. That night, he took Stephanie to dinner, which I wasn't best pleased about, but no more upsets since, and he even gave her role with a few lines of dialogue, which, apparently, she handled very well.'

'Have Rachel and Jacob been involved in the film?'

'Yes, they have been in a couple of crowd scenes, which they enjoyed, especially as they got to meet Julie Pattison and Jeremy Saville.'

'And were they smitten?'

'Not particularly. They're both feet-on-the-ground young people with strong independent characters and not easily impressed, although Rachel did admit to me that she was surprised at Jeremy's sensitivity. Although not especially bright, apparently he's nothing like the boorish drunken idiot the tabloids have portrayed him to be in the past. As for Jacob, he was more interested in talking to the cameramen and costume designers; he's a talented artist and has just completed postgraduate courses in film studies and interior design.'

'Okay, Mrs Croft thanks for your very useful input. We'd better talk to Mr Jennings.'

'We'll see you on Saturday then, Chief Inspector. And please call me Victoria. Mrs Croft makes me feel ancient. You're invited as well, sergeant; feel free to bring a friend.'

Sweeney, having felt left out, swelled visibly and said, 'Thanks, Victoria,' deliberately incurring Parrot's displeasure.

The two policemen headed for the conservatory. As they walked, Sweeney said to his boss, 'Well, you've done it again, Sir.'

'And what exactly is *It*, sergeant?'

'Five minutes ago, a woman screams at us to stop, more or less accuses us of trespassing, and probably imagining worse; then, you speak to her and we're being invited to Saturday brunch to meet her family. Please teach me how to win people over, Sir.'

'I'm not sure that I can. It's not a conscious effort on my part. I just try to be as fair as one can be in this job and treat most people with consideration. Victoria Croft is a classic example of a person under pressure and behaving out of character. I gave her the benefit of the doubt that her initial rant was not customary, but,

The Director's Final Cut

more importantly, Sergeant, remember that most of the time you can achieve more with a few softly spoken words than all the aggressive, confrontational behavior we are surrounded by nowadays. You can't turn the TV on without a constant barrage of extreme conduct spewing out of every channel under the dubious guise of entertainment.'

Sweeney opened the conservatory door onto the terrace where Charles Jennings and John Tapley were throwing insults and punches at each other, the former landing more regularly than the latter by a five-to-one ratio. Sweeney looked at his boss, who said, 'You'd better break it up, Sergeant, or else one or both of us could end up with cracked ribs through excessive laughter.' Sweeney stepped in and swiftly stopped the altercation with not much complaint from either combatant. Parrot then introduced himself and his sergeant and said, 'Right, gentlemen, I think you'd agree that it's far too pleasant a morning for fisticuffs, and someone might get hurt.' He sarcastically added, 'Eventually, so I suggest you shake hands and cool off. The two antagonists raised smiles of sorts, then John Tapley offered his hand and said, 'Absolutely right, Chief Inspector. Sorry, CJ, my fault. Shouldn't be so touchy. Let's have a drink together later.'

Jennings replied, 'No, my fault, Johnny. Damn schedule's got me all tetchy; see you at lunch...drinks on me.'

Tapley wandered off across the lawn, and Charlie Jennings sat down and invited Parrot and Sweeney to join him.

'Would either of you two gentlemen like some tea or coffee or maybe some breakfast?' For a second, Parrot looked interested but fought the urge and declined the director's offer.

'We're here in connection with an injury sustained by Oliver Tapley. What can you tell us about the incident, Mr Jennings?'

'There's not much to tell, Chief Inspector. He was drunk and making unwelcome advances to Julie Pattison. I pulled him off, and he attacked me. So in self-defense I punched him. Is he okay?'

'A broken nose, apparently. Is that why his brother and you were fighting about just now?'

'Good God no. Johnny's long past caring about Oliver's troubled lifestyle. He's been through the ringer so many times he's developed a defense mechanism called indifference, or so he tells everyone, although, personally, I think he still sees himself as his kid brother's protector. Why else would he keep the bum around?'

'Can Ms Pattison verify your account of the incident with Oliver Tapley?'

'I'm positive she can, Mr Parrot.'

'So what were you and John Tapley fighting about just now?'

'What directors and producers always fight about Chief Inspector. Budgets and scheduling. Between you and me, the production is behind schedule. Consequently, we're $1.5 million over budget on our second week.'

'What's the reason for the overshoot, Mr Jennings?'

'The main reason is that we have an inexperienced guy in the male lead who is forcing us to reshoot every scene that he appears in several times over.'

'You're talking about Jeremy Saville?'

'Correct. He's a good looking, capable young actor, but this film is an adaption of a bestseller that has the potential to be huge at the box office. At the moment, he's falling short of my expectations, if not John's.'

'So, would I be right in assuming that Jeremy Saville was not your choice for the male lead?'

'Correct again. As so often happens, there was a trade off. I wanted Julie for the female lead, and the studio wanted another young actress. I dug my heels in and got my way, but, of course, I then had to accept Jeremy Saville.'

'Tell me exactly what you and Mr Tapley were at such odds with that it turned violent.'

'Because I was so against Jeremy for the part, John accused me of deliberately sabotaging the production to prove a point. He said that he and his team thought the guy was doing a great job in the lead and that the constant reshoots were unnecessarily wasteful and were a spiteful act of petulance on my part.'

'What was your reply?'

'I told him that I would never jeopardize his or any-one's production because of a difference of opinion, but that I intended to continue to make the best picture possible. If that meant reshooting scenes until I was sat-isfied, then that is exactly what I would do regardless of budgets. He got agitated, and the rest you saw.'

'Are you and John Tapley friends?'

'Yes, I would call him a friend. We don't see each other that often nowadays. We used to be more of a foursome, John's wife Jane Warren and my second wife are best friends from school days, so when we broke up, that effectively split up the friendship. John and I still get together occasionally and we have remained good friends till this day. Even allowing for what you witnessed earlier.'

'Do you have any contact with Jane Warren? I am right in thinking that she is here with her husband?'

'Yes, she's here, but, sadly, we don't talk. She hasn't forgiven me for the break up, even though it was over seven years ago. Unfortunately, Lizzie, my second wife, took to the bottle after we split up, and Jane had to pick up the pieces. What strange creature's women are, Chief Inspector. Lizzie and I were married for five years. In all that time, I never saw her take a drink; now, if you will excuse me, we are shooting in ten minutes, and I have to make sure my staff have put the cameras in the correct locations.'

'Okay, Mr Jennings, but we will need to speak to you again if Mr Tapley prefers charges.'

'Highly unlikely, Chief Inspector. He probably has no recollection of the incident. Now, if you will excuse me, I really must dash.' With a wave of his hand, Charlie Jennings walked briskly away.

Dan Sweeney turned to his boss. 'Well, Sir, what do you make of our Mr Jennings?'

'Not the most pleasant of men, but what puzzles me is, after watching Jennings and John Tapley's *Handbags at Dawn* display earlier, how the hell did he manage to break Oliver Tapley's nose?'

'Could have just been a lucky punch ? Remember, Tapley was supposedly very drunk.'

'Yes, you're probably right. Anyway, let's get back to the station and try to resume what we're really paid for.'

❖ ❖ ❖

The next few days passed without any further incident. Oliver Tapley refused to press charges, and when Parrot and Sweeney made their daily visits to Hadleigh Hall at the insistence of Oswald Rowley, they found nothing but harmony. On the surface anyway. The tabloid press and every popular magazine from around the world had descended like a plague of locusts on Hadleigh, no doubt fueled by rumors of intrigue and violence on the set of the next blockbuster. There was not a room to be had in any hotel, motel, or bed and breakfast within a ten-mile radius. Hadleigh was well and truly on the map, and the pubs and restaurants were doing a roaring trade. Much to the annoyance of George Parrot. He suddenly found that there was no such thing as a quiet pint at The Feathers. When he had ventured in one evening, he was immediately pestered by reporters offering him large amounts of money to dish the dirt. That evening was a first for George Parrot, nearly a full pint of his favorite ale lying forlornly on the counter, as he trudged moodily back home.

Audrey Parrot took one look at her husband and said, 'Come on, George, I'm taking you out for a nice, quiet meal, and you can tell me all about your horrible day over a glass of wine.'

'A lovely thought, my darling, but we would have to drive to the next county for a quiet meal. Have you seen what's happening to our village?'

'I'm afraid I have. A man approached me as I came out of the butcher's. He wanted to know what your favorite foods were.

'That's going too far. I expect the press on my back, but I won't have you pestered by these parasites.'

'Please don't worry about me, George. For a fleeting moment, it was quite exciting to be approached by a national newspaper...until he asked me about your food preferences.'

'I suppose it was a tabloid newspaper?'

'Yes, he offered me fifty pounds for the information; that's why I offered to take you out to dinner.'

'Audrey, tell me you didn't take the mon—' then, he caught himself mid sentence, as the smirk on his wife's face caused the penny to drop. 'You always get me. Even after all these years, I still fall for it. Do you know something? I wouldn't change it for the world. You're right; we're going out for a nice, quiet meal, even if I have to drive to Scotland.'

In the event, Parrot only had to drive about twenty miles to find a quaint little restaurant with a thatched roof and leaded windows called The Olde Cottage, although it seemed light years from Hadleigh. Over dinner, Parrot asked his wife if she was looking forward to brunch at the Hall on Saturday and to meeting Peter Scarll.

'Very much so.' she replied. 'Since you told me about the invite, I decide to gen up on him. He went through a very bad time about nine years ago. His wife left him for a much younger man, and he was devastated. He had absolutely no idea about their affair until he came home one day to a Dear John letter. He went to pieces, and his music suffered for a few years. He gave an interview recently in which he gave all the credit to his sister and daughter for resurrecting his life and music. The critics say his latest work is the highpoint of his career.'

'Will the film people be there, George?'

'I really don't know, but, judging from what Victoria Croft told me, I don't think Charles Jennings will be getting an invite.'

'Oh, that's a shame. I was quite looking forward to meeting him.'

'You admire his work, I suppose?'

'No, not really. I think he's a bit of a hunk, and I was hoping we could slip off to the woods for some rumpy-pumpy.' Then, looking at the bemused look on her husband's face, she said, 'Of course I admire his work. Young British double Oscar winners are a rare breed and I would like to make my own mind up about him. Men always seem to have a downer on other men who are successful with women.'

'I wouldn't call three broken marriages successful.'

'Stop being obtuse, George; you know what I mean.'

'Remember, I've met him. Believe me, there's not much to recommend.'

'I'm sure you're right, but, from what you tell me, he was under pressure and probably wasn't acting rationally, so I would like the chance to formulate my own opinion.'

'Of course, dear, you're quite right. Would you like a pudding?'

Early Saturday morning, Audrey Parrot had already shown her husband three potential outfits suitable for the festivities at Hadleigh Hall, each of which he had enthused about, but he knew the dreaded question had yet to be asked.

Moments later, it duly arrived. 'Oh, George, help me decide…which outfit do you prefer?'

He looked thoughtful for a moment, then, employing the same tactic he had used for over twenty years, said, 'I like the green one the best.'

'Oh, do you? I thought the light cotton cream two piece was the most suitable, and I can match my shoes and handbag with the cream much easier than the green or the blue outfit.'

'Yes, Audrey, that does make sense. Go for the cream job then,' he said in as neutral a way as possible, having already decided an hour earlier that it was his favorite.

Audrey, now content with her choice, began to address what her husband should wear. Beginning with elimination, she said, 'Now, George, please tell me that you're not going to wear that awful blue blazer and those equally horrible grey flannel trousers again. I nearly gave them to the charity shop a few weeks ago.'

'What's wrong with them? Everybody tells me how smart they look.'

'People did say that, George, but that was twenty years ago; they're ancient and dowdy. I bought you a beautiful yellow linen jacket for your birthday three years ago, which you've never worn. Well, I would like you to put it on today, together with the white shirt I bought you for your last birthday, and the black trousers I bought you last Christmas…oh, and no tie…you're off duty.'

He knew there was little point in protesting. Audrey's taste in fashion and most things was infinitely better than his own, but he did ask her not to throw out his blazer and grey flannels, to which she agreed as long as he wore the outfit of her choice. Satisfied with his small victory, he agreed, albeit reluctantly, to comply with his wife's choices.

They arrived at Hadleigh Hall by cab just before one o'clock, and, although reassured constantly by his wife, George Parrot felt exceedingly uncomfortable in his new set of clothes. He couldn't get the idea out of his head that a senior police officer shouldn't be seen in public wearing a yellow jacket. Sensing his unease, Audrey took his arm, smiled, and said, 'George, you look the bee's knees, and I'm not just saying that because I'm your better half, so please relax and enjoy the day.'

'I'll try,' came the feeble reply.

Arriving at the garden terrace, the Parrot's were greeted by Victoria Croft, who said, 'So glad you could come Chief Inspector, and you must be Audrey, I'm Victoria and I hear you're a fan of my brother's music.'

'Yes, a big fan. George tells me that he's coming for the weekend, and I'd love to meet him.'

'He's actually going to spend a couple of weeks with us. I told him that these film people were getting me down a little, so he offered to keep me company for a while, for which I'm very grateful. Anyway, let's get some drinks organized; then, I'll introduce you to Peter. By the way, Chief Inspector, I think you look very dapper,' which brought a 'told you so' look from Audrey Parrot.

Having sorted out the drinks, Victoria whisked Audrey away, leaving Parrot to amuse himself. He spotted Dan Sweeney talking to Julie Pattison and joined them.

'Afternoon, Sir. I hardly recognized you in that outfit.'

'Parrot, choosing to ignore his sergeant's comments, smiled at Julie Pattison. 'How nice to see you again, even though your choice of company is somewhat questionable.'

'Don't be too hard on Daniel, Mr Parrot; he's been perfectly charming, and I think you look great. Bright colors really suit you, but, if you don't mind me saying, a straw hat would be the perfect finishing touch.'

'I'm sure it would, but I would ask you not to repeat that comment, particularly within earshot of my wife. Is Mr Jennings here this afternoon?'

'No, he and the Tapleys left for London early this morning to meet with the guys who are handling the publicity for the movie. They won't be back till tomorrow afternoon.'

An attractive, suntanned lady suddenly appeared, and, kissing Julie on both cheeks, said, 'Hello, my darling, are you having fun? But of course you are sandwiched between these two handsome hunks. Well, are you going to introduce me?'

'Yes, of course. Mr Parrot, Daniel, say hello to Sheila Pattison, or to put it another way, my mother.'

'Parrot offered his hand. 'Very pleased to meet you, Mrs Pattison. I can see where Julie gets her good looks from.'

Sweeney looked astonished. Was this really his boss, dyed in the wool George Parrot, flattering a member of the opposite sex? His new clothes must have bewitched him, he thought.

'Please call me Sheila. Are you two gentlemen with the film production?'

'No they're not, Mum,' said Julie. 'To give them their proper titles, this is Detective Chief Inspector George Parrot and Detective Sergeant Daniel Sweeney.'

'Are they your personal bodyguards, my darling?'

'Of course not. You'll have to excuse my mother; she's lived in America for too long.'

'Not at all, my darling daughter. You're a major star now, and you should have police protection, especially with all the screwballs out there.'

'Mother, this is a quiet suburb of leafy England...not crazy California.'

Parrot turned to Sheila Pattison. 'Please don't worry yourself on that score, Sheila. Sergeant Sweeney and I have been commissioned by people in high places to look after Julie while she's staying here.'

'That's very comforting, George. Oh, you don't mind me calling you George, I hope?'

'Not at all, Sheila. We British are not formal all the time.'

Sweeney thought, *not just compliments, but he's actually flirting with her. There has to be some sort of spell on his new clothes.*

'Are you here in England visiting Julie?' asked Parrot.

'I'm actually staying with old friends of mine just outside London, and I drove down for the day to see my daughter.'

'What she really means is that she's here to keep tabs on me,' said Julie.

'You know that's not true. You're more sensible than I've ever been. Never given me a moment's trouble, George; she's was born mature.'

'How long have you lived in America, Sheila?' Sweeney enquired.

'Over twenty years. Julie was just a baby when I emigrated…best move I ever made.'

'You've retained your English accent, though.'

'Deliberate effort on my part. The British are highly thought of in the States, and my voice has played a part in opening many doors.'

Julie sighed and said, 'Come on, Daniel, let's get some food. I feel all our yesterdays could be brewing.'

'You two run along. George and I can amuse ourselves,' Sheila said flirtatiously.

'Can I get you a drink?' asked Parrot, sensing a slight change in Sheila Pattison's demeanor

'No thanks, but I would like to seriously ask you if you think my daughter is in any danger?'

'None whatsoever as far as I know. Why? Do you wish to tell me something?'

'It's nothing more than a feeling, really, but, since she's been seeing Charlie Jennings, I've been worried sick. The man is successful, talented, and very charming when he has to be. But it's veneer. Underneath, he's a cruel and selfish person, George. Believe me. I'm not some hysterical mother prone to irrational feelings. I've had to play the game to get where I am, and I've done things I'm not particularly proud of, but I was a young, single mother in a strange country with no family or friends for support, if that's an excuse, but I am not a willful person unlike Jennings. Oh, he's sweetness and light when things are going his way, but he's ruined people's lives without compunction.'

'What is your business, Sheila?'

'I run a celebrity agency in Los Angeles.'

'Is Julie a client?'

'From an early age. In fact, I owe her my success. You see, when I first arrived in the States, I struggled to make ends meet. I was working as a waitress. One day, a very nice lady came into the restaurant, took one look at Julie, and said she would be perfect for a commercial she was arranging for a client. We got talking and hit it off. Next thing, I'm working in her agency. Over the next five years, she taught me all there was to know about the business. More importantly, she introduced me to every contact she'd ever made. She treated me and Julie like the daughter and granddaughter she never had. When she passed away two years ago, it was the saddest day of my life. So, you see, George, I'm living proof that America really is the land of opportunity.'

'What a wonderful story, Sheila. You should write a book about your life.'

'Already have. Two large publishing firms are competing for the rights as we speak.'

'Is it very salacious?'

'Extremely. After all, it's what sells newspapers and books these days…throw in some confrontation, real or otherwise, for good measure, and, bingo! We're talking bestseller,' she said with a hearty laugh.

'Excuse me for saying this, but Julie seems very level headed to get involved with someone like Jennings.'

'No, you're analysis is spot on, but, remember, the Dr Jekyll side of him is very engaging.'

'So are you saying that Julie hasn't seen him turn into Mr Hyde?'

'I think she's seen enough to know their relationship won't work. I give it a few weeks.'

'Really? Has Julie spoken about to you about any doubts she may have.'

'Good lord no. That's not her way, but I know my daughter, and the signs are there. Trust me, George, a few weeks. Anyway, he's much too old for her. She wants a big family, and I can't see Charlie boy fulfilling that role. Besides, the strong rumor is that he's sterile. I mean, he's been married three times and has no offspring.'

'Just changing the subject, Sheila, has Julie knowledge of self-defense?'

'You bet she has. Tough town like L.A., I made sure she could look after herself. Why do you ask?'

'No sinister motive. She just looks very fit. What's she in to, Jujitsu or Karate?'

'Neither, though she's tried both. Her passion is Tai Chi, and she's a black belt, so tell that sergeant of yours to mind his manners.'

'Talking of which, I see that he and Julie are talking to my wife, Audrey, and Victoria Croft. Shall we join them?'

'Fed up with my company already?'

'Quite the reverse, I can assure you, but I don't want to be accused of monopolizing the most attractive woman here today, with the exception of my wife, of course.'

Sheila Pattison took Parrot's arm as they began to walk towards the small group. 'I hope Audrey is not the jealous type, George?'

'Good gracious no, not a possessive bone in her body,' he said, trying to sound more certain than he really believed.

Victoria waved to them and said, 'Come on, you two, we're going inside now to hear Peter play some of his new composition.'

Parrot smiled and said, 'Wonderful, what a treat.' He was actually more interested in the spectacular looking buffet, having been denied his usual Saturday morning fry-up on the grounds that Audrey was far too busy getting ready and that she didn't want to arrive at Hadleigh Hall smelling of bacon and cooking oil. In the event, Peter Scarll only played for thirty minutes. Even the starving Parrot had to admit that it really had been a treat. Shortly after, having demolished two platefuls of delicious English fare, Parrot felt particularly well disposed to life. Especially as he had spotted a barrel of 'Trooper's Folly', his favorite ale, which he was now keenly sampling.' Audrey appeared with a stunning looking lady whom he recognized as Jane Warren.

'Very nice to meet you, Chief Inspector. Audrey tells me that you're the good cop in the routine.'

'Well, she may be slightly biased, but I thank her all the same,' Parrot said, giving his wife a look of false appreciation. 'I hear your husband and his brother have gone to London with Mr Jennings.'

'I knew John and Oliver were scheduled to meet the guys they've hired for the film's publicity campaign, but I didn't know Jennings was involved, but, there again, what doesn't he get involved in?'

'He did tell me that he is persona non grata as far as you're concerned.'

'An overdramatic conclusion on his part. I'm actually quite indifferent towards the callous, two-timing, odious bastard,' she said, throwing her head back and letting out a raucous laugh.

Parrot and Audrey joined in the laughter, although he couldn't help feeling that, as funny as her tirade had been, there was a prowling sense of animosity present.

'He also told me the reason why you fell out,' Parrot said sympathetically.

'I'm sure the potted version he gave you was very succinct and to the point. But, believe me, watching your best friend turn into a pitiful alcoholic wreck before your very eyes is far removed from his "get on with your life" attitude.'

'Has she fully recovered?'

'Thankfully, yes. She's now married to a lovely man, has a two-year-old daughter, and is about to resurrect her career in a play on Broadway.'

'What about your career, Jane?' Audrey said. 'Don't you miss the success and the adulation?'

'If I'm totally honest, I would have to say sometimes. But, you know, I've never been under any illusions about my acting ability. I was a pretty good hoofer who got lucky enough to appear in a few very good movies. My life now with John and the kids is far more rewarding.'

'Have you been watching any of the filming?' asked Parrot.

'I've seen a few scenes, but Jennings gets paranoid if they're too many people on the set, so I deliberately stay away.'

'Have you formed any impressions?'

'Julie Pattison is a fantastic talent. I'm sure she's going to be a huge star, and she's such a lovely down-to-earth person, which makes her relationship with Jennings all the harder to fathom.'

'Have you spoken to her about what he did to your friend?'

'No, I would never get involved with someone else's personal life.'

'Do you know Julie's mother?'

'Sheila? Sure, we go way back. She was my agent; well, I'll rephrase that—she is my agent, as she continually tells me, and when I'm ready to return to acting, she'll be waiting.'

'How would you critique Jeremy Saville's acting ability?'

'I'm impressed. He's a bit green, but he's not over-awed, and he's doing a great job. Remember, although he's the male lead, this is an adaption of a Winifred Creamer bestseller and is all about the heroine, as are all her books. Have you met her? She's an absolute treasure, an unashamed feminist with a wicked sense of humor.'

'Jane's right,' said Audrey. 'Victoria introduced me to her earlier, and she had us all in fits.'

'So, Jeremy's character is secondary compared to that of Julie's?'

'Very much so,' Jane replied. 'He plays Simon Mulberry, a captain of a cavalry regiment who falls madly in love with Julie's character, a young girl called Laura Lyons, who happens to be engaged to a local wealthy landowner, who is twenty years her senior, and, of course, a scoundrel. The early part of the story revolves around their first meeting and subsequent love affair. Then, he is sent to the Crimea. When reports reach England of the devastating loss of the six hundred, she is distraught and faces a dilemma. Her family is pressuring her to marry, but she refuses, breaks off the engagement, and flees to London, where she applies for the post of governess to a sweet young girl whose mother has died. I won't bore you with the rest of the story; but, needless to say, there is a happy ending, but not before Laura has to deal with all sorts of difficult situations. So you can see, the story is a bit like Elizabeth Bennett meets Jane Eyre, and Winifred, like Jane Austen and Charlotte Bronte, excels at giving her female characters a sense of purpose and independence. It's a great part for Julie and one that will make her a big star.'

'And Winifred has written the screenplay, I believe?' asked Parrot.

'You're damned right Winifred has,' came the retort directly behind Parrot. He turned to find a diminutive figure in a tweed outfit with permed grey hair and a craggy face that reminded him of the late Margaret Rutherford.

'I suppose you're the Inspector chappie?' Without waiting for Parrot to respond, she continued, 'Thought so. Always can spot a copper; it's the eyes, you know— they're never still, always on the move. Mind you, Audrey did point you out to me earlier.'

'Well, I'm very pleased to meet you', Parrot finally managed to say.

'Same here, Chief Inspector. Have to say, though, I probably wouldn't have booked you for a rozzer, not with that lemon jacket on anyway. Is that Trooper's Folly you're drinking by the way?'

'Yes it is. Would you care for a glass? I was just about ready for a refill.'

'I certainly would. A pint, mind you, in a straight glass. Can't abide drinking beer from a thick rimmed jug.'

'A lady after my own heart...I'll just be a minute. Give me a hand, would you, Daniel?'

'I'll come with you,' said Julie Pattison. 'I need a re-fill, too. Can I get anyone else a drink?' A chorus of 'No Thank Yous' rang out, so the actress with a policeman on each arm headed for the beer tent.

They arrived at the bar, and Parrot ordered the drinks and said, 'You know, Julie, you didn't have to a chaperone us. I wasn't going to talk shop with Daniel.'

'Oh yes you were. I'm afraid the look on Audrey's face gave you away when you asked Daniel for a hand.'

'Okay, Julie, you win, but I was going to talk small kiosk rather than shop,' Parrot said, laughing as usual at his own brand of humor. He then abruptly said knowingly, 'that must have been a honey of a punch you threw to have broken Oliver Tapley's nose.'

'Yes, it was, but it was a straight arm rather than a punch. How did you know?'

'Daniel and I saw your fiancé and John Tapley's laughable excuse for a punch up; then, your mother told me about your passion for Tai Chi. It wasn't difficult to work out the rest, and I'm assuming everyone agreed to a cover up story?'

'You really are very astute, Chief Inspector, but I must correct you on one tiny error.'

'I'm intrigued. Please tell me, what did I get wrong?'

'When you referred jokingly to the punch up, you should have said ex-fiancé. Shall we head back?'

Parrot nodded and said, 'Yes, of course,' then added. 'Daniel, would you mind taking this pint back to Winifred? I'm sure she's spitting feathers by now. We'll join you in a couple of minutes. I just want a brief word with Julie.'

Sweeney reluctantly complied, albeit with a smile, for he would have rather been the one alone with Julie on hearing the news of the break up.

'I suppose you're going to tell me what a lucky escape I've had,' Julie said. Parrot smiled. 'Now who's being astute? But, yes, and I think you'll find it's a pretty widely held view. I really don't want to pry, but I'm going to. Was there a particular reason for the split?'

'No. I told him a few weeks ago that it was over, but we agreed to keep it to ourselves until the movie was finished.'

'What made you tell Daniel and myself then?'

'I'd rather not say just now, if you don't mind, Chief Inspector.'

'Of course I don't. Just my professional curiosity, that's all. Let's get back and hear some more from Winifred; they certainly don't make them like her anymore.'

The mood between them had changed, and they strolled back in silence to the others whose ranks had been swollen by the arrival of Peter Scarll and Rachel Croft.

'Ah, there you are, Chief Inspector,' said Winifred Creamer jovially. 'Jolly good ale, this Trooper's Folly. Did you know that it was created by Walter Stoddart, a cousin of mine?'

'Really?' replied Parrot. 'Do you get free supplies?'

'I only wish I did, but no. The truth is that it was his only worthwhile contribution in an otherwise mundane existence. He sold the formula for a pittance; then, rather poetically, drunk himself to death. Still, it's a legacy of sorts, I suppose.'

Changing the subject, Parrot asked her how she thought the film was coming along.

'Haven't the foggiest idea,' she said. 'I was promised faithfully that they would stay true to my screenplay and the spirit of the book, but you know what these transatlantic types are like. Wouldn't surprise me if Laura ends up with a South Carolina accent and a black maid and Simon turns out to be a carpetbagger.'

Now in full sway, Winifred with the Trooper's Folly well and truly kicking in, continued to hold court and amuse everyone for the next five minutes until, suddenly, in midstream, she turned and walked away. With an exaggerated wave of the hand, she said, 'Sorry must go. There's Deirdre Somerset, and she owes me fifty quid.'

When the laughing had died down, Victoria Croft introduced Parrot to her brother, and his immediate impression was that of a painfully shy man who avoided eye contact and a voice that barely rose above a whisper. Rachel Croft, on the other hand, was the antithesis of her uncle. She greeted Parrot with a firm handshake and a strong, confident voice, much akin to those of her mother. She eyed Parrot for a moment, then said, 'I'm thinking about a career in the police service, Mr Parrot, but I'm concerned that my gender will inhibit my advancement. What do you think?'

A very clever and loaded question, thought Parrot, at the same time doubting she had any intention of such a profession. 'Well, Rachel, if you're serious, I'll not give you a stock answer. There are many more women in the service nowadays, which I believe is very positive, but, in percentage terms, they still lag way behind men in the top jobs. That's not to say you should take that as a deterrent; after all, the present home secretary is a woman.'

'Is that relevant? After all, the home secretary is a political appointment,' Rachel said seriously.

'Well, maybe you should also consider a career in politics,' Parrot said with some alacrity.

'Rachel, in the police service or politics…don't make me laugh,' said Jacob Scarll, joining the group.

'Come on, children, play nicely,' said Victoria Croft. 'And Mr Parrot is off duty. He's here to relax and enjoy himself.'

'That's perfectly okay,' said Parrot. 'Rachel, if you are in earnest, I know quite a few senior women police officers who would be only too pleased to give you the inside track.'

'Is your daughter not here today, Peter?' Audrey said, sensing a sudden stiffness within the group, changing the subject.

'No, Stephanie is staying the weekend with an old school friend. She'll be back on Monday,' said Victoria, before her brother had a chance to reply.

'Oh, what a pity. I would have liked to have met her.'

'Well, come to lunch on Wednesday then, Audrey. It's going to be an all women thing, and Stephanie will be there,' said Victoria. 'I'm sure if enough of us ask him, Peter will play some more of his latest work.'

'I'd love to, Victoria, thanks very much,' Audrey said appreciatively.

The afternoon drifted pleasantly into early evening, and the Parrots took their leave. In the cab on the way home, Audrey snuggled up to her husband and said, 'What a lovely day, George, so different from our normal Saturday. Oh, sorry, that came out wrong, but you know what I mean.'

'Yes, dear, I know what you mean. A very good crowd. Winifred's hilarious, isn't she? Although I have to say Peter Scarll is the most timid man I think I've ever met.'

'I was talking to him one to one, and he was absolutely fine,' Audrey countered, 'but Victoria told me that he doesn't do so well in a crowd.'

'You like Victoria, don't you?'

'Very much. She's very solid. Look at the way she protects her family, especially Peter. I'd like to think we will become good friends. She told me about your first meeting when she mistook you and Daniel for trespassers. She said the indignant look on your face was priceless,' said Audrey, laughing.

'Speaking of my sergeant, did you notice that he spent the whole afternoon with Julie Pattison before the pair of them slipped away?'

'Yes, I did, and so did everyone else. I think it's lovely.'

'Not the word I'd choose, and I think a fatherly word to him on Monday morning is in order.'

'Don't you dare, George. Let them enjoy themselves. He won't thank you for interfering.'

'Maybe you're right, but a dreamy-eyed sergeant is something I can do without.'

'Daniel doesn't strike me as dreamy eyed, George; in fact, quite the opposite from what you've told me about him.'

'That's as well as maybe, but you know the expression about playing with fire.'

'Come on, George, out with it. You're concerned for the lad, aren't you?'

'I've seen the way he looks at her, and it's not as if she's here to stay. In a couple of months, she'll be back in the States or making another film in some exotic location, and I doubt very much that she will be reminiscing about a village sergeant. Their worlds are light years apart, and he's going to get hurt.'

'I doubt that very much, George. They're just having fun, and I can't see Daniel treating this as a big romance, so stop worrying about the boy; he'll be fine.'

'I suppose you're right,' said Parrot, closing the issue, although still intending to speak to his sergeant.

Early Monday morning, Parrot duly called Sweeney into his office and tactfully, or as tactfully as George Parrot was able, raised his concerns about the relationship without appearing too worried on a personal level. Sweeney smiled and said, 'No problem. Julie and I get on really well, but I'm under no illusions about anything permanent. I thank you for your interest, Sir.'

Parrot suddenly wished he'd taken Audrey's advice and left well enough alone and quickly changed the subject. 'When are you going to take your inspector exams,

Daniel? You've been a detective sergeant for about five years. Time for promotion, don't you think?' he said formally.

'It's been on my mind for a while now. I'd value your honest opinion, Sir, am I inspector material?'

'I wouldn't have asked you about the exams if I didn't think you capable, but I sense there is something else stopping you taking them.'

'I don't want to move away from the area, Sir. I grew up here, and all my family and friends are local. If I pass the exam, I'll get posted to god knows where.'

'Not necessarily. There are three or four stations within a thirty-mile radius.'

Sweeney thought hard for a moment. The truth was that he enjoyed working with Parrot and didn't want to break up the partnership, but how could he tell him without sounding sycophantic.

'The truth is, Sir, I want to be an inspector, but I would prefer to continue working with you for another couple of years to gain experience before moving on, but I know that the chief constable wouldn't allow a chief inspector to work with another inspector.'

'No, you're quite right, he wouldn't, but he would probably allow an inspector to work with a chief superintendent, especially if said superintendent was supposedly his top man.'

'That's fantastic, Sir, congratulations. You thoroughly deserve it. I'll put in for my exams straight away.'

'Just hold your horses for a second, Sergeant. I haven't accepted yet, and nobody but you, me, and the chief constable knows about the offer...not even Audrey, so not a word or I'll see that you get shipped to somewhere particularly unpleasant when you are an inspector.'

'Of course not, Sir; mum's the word, but why haven't you accepted?'

'Do you recall the other day when I was talking about not being political and playing for headlines? Well, a promotion like this moves me one step nearer to a world I detest. If I can't control my life and life-style, I would rather jack it in now and take early retirement.'

'Forgive me for saying this, Sir, but I think you're allowing your dislike of manipulation and politics to cloud your judgment about what is, after all, a well-deserved reward for hard work and success. Anyway, I don't see you changing your attitude towards those things, even if they were to make you home secretary, and I'm not just saying this because I have a vested interest. It's truly that there should be more of your kind up there making a difference.'

'Well thank you Daniel. I appreciate your sentiments.'

'When do you have to give the chief constable an answer, Sir?'

'By the end of the week. I can tell you that he was none too pleased when I asked for time to think it over. He said, "Good God, man, what's there to think about? A promotion, extra pay, and vacations!" Then, he suggested I check out the difference between a chief superintendent's pension and that of a chief inspector's. He then said that plenty of good men out there would jump at the chance. Then I was summarily dismissed.'

'Do you think Mrs Parrot will be pleased?'

'On the whole, yes; she shares my dislike of controlling and being controlled, but she has always supported my decisions in the past, even though I suspect she hasn't agreed with all of them. Right, let's move on. Major decision time, sergeant.'

'What's that, Sir?'

'Do we have breakfast now, before we go to Hadleigh Hall, or skip breakfast for a brunch at the pub? Either way, it's your turn to pay.'

That evening, Parrot told Audrey about his promotion and voiced his fears about a whole new world. Her response was almost identical to Sweeney's...not that he told her. She finished by saying what he'd expected her to say, namely, 'George, whatever decision you make, I'm behind you one hundred percent.'

Parrot knew that Audrey, for all her downplaying, was thrilled at the news, and he decided to accept the position. After all, he rationalized, there really was a big difference in pension, and, as they had always talked about traveling when he did retire, the added income would ensure they did it in some style.

The following morning, he rang Oswald Rowley and said that he would be delighted to accept the position, to which came the rather gruff reply, 'I should think so, too.' He then said, 'How's everything up at the Hall? You and Sweeney are still looking in every day, I hope?'

'Yes, Sir, as you requested.'

'Good. A bit of high profile policing never hurts.'

'No, Sir,' said Parrot, shaking his head.

'Oh, and by the way, Parrot, a little bird tells me that you and Sweeney attended a garden party there on Saturday.'

'Yes, Sir. Victoria Croft, the owner of the Hall, kindly invited us,' said Parrot, sensing a slight edge to Rowley's comment.

'Oh well, very good. Keep me informed of any developments,' Rowley said briskly before hanging up.

Parrot got the distinct impression that Chief Constable Oswald Rowley was peeved at not getting an invite, but he just chuckled to himself, and then murmured under his breath, 'Unbelievable.'

❖ ❖ ❖

The following day, Audrey went to Hadleigh Hall for the Ladies' Lunch. That evening over dinner, she proceeded to tell her husband about the get together.

'You know, George, I thought it was impossible for a dozen women to be in the same room for three hours without an element of sniping or bitchiness at some stage. Well, today proved me quite wrong. Everybody got on so well, and I got to meet Stephanie.'

'Is she like her father?' asked Parrot.

'Oh, George, she's an absolute angel. Very quiet like Peter, and the family absolutely dote on her, particularly Victoria, who treats her like a second daughter.'

'Did Peter play some more of his work?'

'No. That was the only downside to the day. Victoria said that he wasn't feeling well and was resting in his room and that he asked her to apologize to everyone and promised to play at the next lunch.'

'Doesn't surprise me. He looked a bit peaky on Saturday.'

'Yes, I thought so as well. Victoria told me that he's not very strong, and the strain of composing his latest work had taken its toll. She also told me that she was determined to get him to stay on at the Hall, at least until her brother, Steven, returned from his Caribbean sojourn and possibly longer so that she could look after him properly. She really is a lovely person, so caring and protective towards all her family.'

'Was Winifred there?'

'Oh, yes, larger than life, as usual. She did tell me in one of her quieter moments how her family and he Scarlls have been close friends for generations; she's Victoria's Godmother, you know, and it was she that suggested Hadleigh Hall for the film's central location. She sends her regards to you and looks forward to having a couple of pints of Trooper's Folly with you at the next bash, as she put it.'

'Who else was there?'

'Jane Warren and her two daughters...lovely, well-behaved girls they are, too. Julie and Sheila Pattison, Rachel, of course, and a couple of Victoria's friends.'

'I thought Sheila was staying with friends?'

'Up till yesterday she was. Victoria invited her to stay at the Hall for a few days before she flies back to the States, a nice gesture, I thought.'

'Was Julie not required for filming today then?'

'She started shooting scenes at five o'clock this morning and had finished by midday.'

'So it sounds like a good time was had by all.'

'Yes, it was fun, but there was something not quite right. I can't put my finger on it, just a feeling that everyone was trying a little bit too hard to be jolly.'

'Who exactly was trying too hard?' Parrot said with interest.

'Well, maybe not everyone, but Victoria and Rachel to start with. I don't know what's happened, but each of them was pumped up, and I noticed both of them giving Stephanie what seemed like looks of encouragement, but I could be wrong. I hardly know them, after all, but I'm sure that Sheila and Julie were not on the best of terms. They were perfectly friendly to everybody else, but they were quite obviously not speaking to each other. I noticed it almost immediately. We were in a small group, and there was no eye contact between them, and things hadn't improved by the time I left.'

'Oh well, you know what us coppers say, don't you?' said Parrot jovially.

'No, George, but I'm sure you're about to tell me.'

'Don't get involved with domestic disputes. If you do, be prepared for—'

'Yes, I know, Chief Inspector, be prepared for one, or both, or all of them to turn on you,' interrupted Audrey. 'But, as I have no intention of getting involved, that maxim is totally irrelevant in this instance, isn't it?' she continued tersely.

'I'm sorry if I've upset you. I was just trying to make light of the situation, that's all.'

'I know you were, George, and I'm sorry, too. You're right; it's not my business to get involved in, so let's change the subject.'

'Good idea. What's for pudding?' Parrot said with a broad grin.

The following morning at six thirty, Parrot was awakened by the shrill ring of his bedside telephone. He took the call, and said tersely, 'This had better be important.'

Daniel Sweeney replied, 'It is. Charles Jennings has been murdered. He was found in his trailer a short while ago, with a knife thrust deep into the back of his neck.'

'Okay, Sergeant, I'll see you there in half an hour. Get uniform down there pronto. When this leaks, the press will be swarming all over the place.'

Parrot arrived at the Hall and headed straight to the trailer where Sweeney met him. 'I've phoned forensics. Dr. Starkey and his team are on their way, as is the chief constable, I'm afraid, Sir.'

'Oh, Lord, that's all we need. Well, let's take a look at the body before he arrives.'

'He's been stabbed in the back of the neck with a small knife, and it's been driven in with some force, right up to the hilt, Sir.'

The contorted look on Jennings's face would have done any horror movie director proud. Parrot noted that there was minimal blood loss and thought that death would have been almost instantaneous. The two policemen also noted an empty bottle of expensive red wine, together with an almost empty claret glass, on the director's desk.

'Look at the handle and the hilt, Sergeant. What does that tell us?'

'Well, Sir, it doesn't appear to be a standard kitchen knife.'

'Very good, carry on,' said Parrot encouragingly.

'Well, it looks more like a souvenir, something you might buy in a gift shop perhaps.'

'Excellent. You're on the right track. Think practical, not ornamental.'

'It's a letter opener,' Sweeney said with gusto.

'First class, Sergeant. Now what else can we deduce from the weapon?'

'That, if it belonged to Jennings, the murder was not premeditated; I mean, who chooses a letter opener to commit a deliberate murder?'

'Exactly, and I wouldn't mind betting that it belongs in that fancy walnut box on his desk, part of a set probably,' surmised Parrot.

'So, if he had been opening his mail, he may have forgotten to put it back in the box, and it was picked up at random by the killer,' said Sweeney enthusiastically.

Something along those lines,' said Parrot, deep in thought.

'Considerable force was used to plunge it that far into Jennings' neck, Sir.'

'Indeed, Sergeant, a violent act of deep hatred, if I'm not mistaken.'

'Do you think a woman would have the strength?'

'Undoubtedly, especially one roused to such an emotional pitch, and there's no shortage of women who fit that particular bill, who happen to be staying at the Hall right now. Okay, sergeant, you know the drill. Set up an incident room and organize statements from everyone staying at the Hall; that includes the Tapleys,

Jane Warren, and all the film crew, but you can leave Victoria Croft and Peter and Stephanie Scarll—I'll look after them myself,' said Parrot, who suddenly heard the booming voice of Chief Constable Oswald Rowley, who was being his usual impatient self.

'Where is Chief Inspector Parrot?'

'He's in the director's trailer with Sergeant Sweeney, Sir,' said the harassed-looking young constable.

'Well, what are you waiting for? Go and tell him I need to speak with him urgently.'

'Morning, Sir,' Parrot said, emerging from the trailer. 'Thought I heard your voice.'

'Let's take a walk, Chief Inspector,' Rowley said, and proceeded to head off towards the lawn area at the front of the hall, leaving Parrot trailing in his wake. Reaching a secluded spot well out of earshot, he turned and said, 'Well, George, you know what this means.'

'Yes, Sir, Fleet Street will be here in even greater numbers,' said Parrot.

'Forget Fleet Street, George. The world's media will be coming to Hadleigh; every network news channel and every national newspaper are on their way here, and they will be scrutinizing us under a microscope.' *If they can find somewhere to stay*, thought Parrot. 'I've already spoken to the home secretary,' continued Rowley and I suggested we hold a news conference this morning at eleven o'clock, to which she agreed. Very important times, George; the eyes of the world's press, remember.'

'Yes, Sir. I understand,' Parrot said, understanding only too well.

'Good man. Keep me in touch with any developments. It's important for us to be seen making headway. I'm counting on you, George.'

Parrot headed back to find that Dr. Harry Starkey and his forensic team had arrived.

'Morning, George. See Rowley's here already. I bet he's rubbing his hands together with relish,' Starkey said with disdain.

'Morning, Harry. Yes he is. He called me George at least three times, and he's holding a press conference at eleven, so anything you can tell me by then would be appreciated.'

Starkey smiled at his friend. 'Sure, *George,*' he said, emphasizing the "George", 'I'll get started straight away.'

Sweeney told Parrot that Victoria Croft had offered the use of the library and the study as temporary interview rooms and was organizing some coffee and breakfast for everyone.

'How was she? Did she seem on edge?'

'No, not at all. She was very calm and in control. I told her that you would be taking statements from her. Peter, Stephanie, and she seemed quite relaxed. She did ask if you could leave her brother till last as he was feeling unwell and was still asleep.'

'Very well. Oh, and on reflection, I think I'd better interview Julie Pattison as well.'

'Yes, Sir, that's probably for the best,' Sweeney said as professionally as he could.

Parrot went directly to the library, where Victoria Croft was waiting. He was pleased to see breakfast had arrived before him in the shape of a couple of bacon sandwiches and proceeded to tuck into them at Victoria's invitation.

'I feel awkward,' she said. 'I don't know whether to call you Chief Inspector or George.'

'Let's not worry too much about names or titles at the moment,' Parrot said kindly. 'But, we do have to ask everyone at the Hall to account for their movements from last night until this morning.'

'Of course. I went to bed around eleven and slept soundly until six fifteen, when I was awoken by banging on the front door. I went down to find one of the film crew in an agitated state, shouting that Jennings was dead and asking me to call the police, which I did straight away.'

'Was anyone else up at that time?'

'Yes, Julie Pattison had been in her trailer being made up for a scene that they were due to shoot early this morning, and Winifred was in the kitchen having breakfast.'

'So Winifred stayed here last night?'

'Yes, she quite often does. She has her own room, and when it gets late, we always encourage her to stay, rather than ride that old rickety bicycle of hers back to her cottage.'

Parrot thought what a genuinely nice person Victoria was. Obviously, the invitation to stay was real enough but much more likely because the old girl was in no condition to ride her bike, a fact that Victoria felt was best left out. How very commendable, Parrot thought.

'Did you see Peter and Stephanie this morning?'

'Peter has been feeling unwell since yesterday morning and has been in his room since then and I woke

Stephanie about fifteen minutes ago to tell her the news.'

'How did she react?'

'She's very upset, of course.'

'And what about you? Are you upset?'

'I can't lie to you and pretend I'm upset; he was a despicable individual.'

'Did you kill him, Victoria?' Parrot asked, deliberately making steadfast eye contact.

'No, I did not kill him, Chief Inspector, and that is the God's honest truth,' she said unflinchingly.

'I believe you; yet, I believe someone in this house did kill him, and I would caution you that if there is any light you can shed on this murder to do so now, irrespective of friend or family loyalty. I need to know.'

'I truly know nothing about Jennings' murder,' Victoria said with conviction.

'That's all for now then. I'd like to see Stephanie next. Could you ask her to come in, in about five minutes?'

'Go easy on her, please; she's a delicate creature.'

'Yes, of course,' Parrot said, while thinking about the way she had forthrightly phrased her answer about Jennings' untimely demise. She didn't kill him, he thought, but she knows a good deal more than she's letting on.

Stephanie demurely entered the room as Parrot was just polishing off the last of the bacon sandwiches. 'Ah, there you are, Stephanie. Very pleased to meet you at last. I believe you met my wife Audrey yesterday,' Parrot said, at the same time noticing what an extremely attractive young lady she was.

'Yes, I did. She's very nice,' Stephanie said in a quiet voice.

'Now, as your aunt has told you, Mr Jennings has been murdered, and my team and I need to question everyone as to their movements between late last night and this morning,' Parrot said in a deliberately low key.

'I went to bed around eleven and read for about an hour, then slept till Aunt Vicky woke me a little while ago.'

'So you didn't leave your room after eleven o'clock?'

'No.'

'You didn't get up to go to the bathroom or to the kitchen for a drink?'

'No.'

'I believe you went to dinner with Charles Jennings a couple of weeks ago.'

'Yes, he took me out for a meal, and then we went to the cinema.'

'Did you like him?'

'Yes, he was very nice.'

'Forgive me for asking, Stephanie; were your feelings towards him any deeper?'

'Yes, I was fond of him, but he was more like an uncle.'

'Did you see him more than once?'

'We went out for a drive one evening and stopped for a drink.'

'Ok, Stephanie, that's all for now,' Parrot said. 'You missed a grand day last Saturday. Your aunt told me you went to stay with an old school friend for the weekend.'

'Yes, that's right,' she said...rather sheepishly, Parrot thought.

'When you have a moment, would you give my sergeant the name, address, and telephone number of your friend?'

'Is that really necessary?'

'I would appreciate your cooperation. Is there a problem?'

'No, of course not. I'll get them straight away.'

'Good, will you ask your aunt to come back in, please?'

Victoria returned shortly after, and Parrot said, 'Has a doctor been called to see your brother?'

'No, although our family doctor is aware of Peter's condition. A few days rest and he'll be fine.'

'Is he well enough to answer a few questions?'

'I think so, but maybe you could interview him in his room.'

'Yes, of course,' Parrot said, then added, 'but, in the meantime, let him sleep, and I'll question him this afternoon, when hopefully he's a little stronger.'

'Thank you so much, George; that's very kind and much appreciated,' Victoria said sincerely. 'If you would like some more bacon sandwiches, there are mounds of them in the dining room or I can get the cook to rustle you up a full English breakfast; Audrey did mention that you were a breakfast person.'

'Did she now?' said a smiling Parrot. 'It's not good for members of the public to know a detective's weaknesses. I shall be having a word with my dear wife this evening, but I suppose I could force down another couple of sandwiches.'

A replete Parrot caught up with Dr. Starkey at the murder scene. 'Anything for me yet, Harry?'

'Time of death, between eleven p.m. and two a.m., attacked from behind, and the killer was right handed. As you know, considerable force was used, and death was instant. Give you a more detailed report this afternoon, after we get him on the slab.'

'Thanks, Harry, that's great. Have you seen our friend Rowley by chance?'

'Seen him? He's done nothing but pester me and the team since we arrived. Keeps saying things like "best efforts, people" and "we're all under pressure on this one" and "no cock-ups, please."'

'Do you know where he is now?' Parrot said without a great deal of interest.

'I can answer that,' said the arriving Dan Sweeney. 'He's getting ready for his press conference. Listen to this, he's got the film's head make-up artist to give him a makeover; he's actually ensconced in Julie's trailer.'

'Come on, Sergeant; this I've got to see,' said Parrot.

'Me too. He asked me to keep him in touch,' said the doctor, and all three headed for the trailer.

Parrot opened the door of the trailer without knocking and had to use every ounce of self control at the sight before him, for there was Chief Constable Oswald Rowley being pampered by two female make-up artists and resembling a renegade from the Mikado.

'Excuse me, Sir, just thought I'd let you know that we've completed our initial interviews and that we're making progress, but maybe this is not a good time. I'll bring you up to date after the press briefing.'

'Yes, do that, George. And remember, you're my top man, and I'm relying on you for an early result on this one.'

'Yes Sir. Dr. Starkey is here, Sir, and wants a quick word,' said Parrot, not wishing his friend to forego the visual pleasure enjoyed by himself.

'Come in, Harry,' said Rowley. 'What have you got for me?'

'Sorry, Daniel, but you're far too young to endure such a harrowing sight,' Parrot told his disappointed sergeant. 'So let us compare notes instead.' Sweeney's initial interviews with Jane Warren, Sheila Pattison, and Winifred Creamer did not appear to throw much light on the murder. All three said that they had gone to bed between eleven and midnight and had slept soundly until this morning. Jane Warren was awakened around six o'clock by one of her daughters, and Winifred took her morning constitutional as she called, it also around six.

'Where are the Tapley brothers?' asked Parrot.

'They spent the night in London. Jane broke the news to her husband this morning, and they should be back around eleven.'

'Are they catching the train?'

'No, they drove down yesterday in John Tapley's car.'

'So either one or both of them could have driven here in the early hours, killed Jennings, then returned to London,' theorized Parrot.

'The main gates to the Hall would have been closed, Sir.'

'They're electronic gates, so find out from Victoria if the Tapleys have the code or a remote control.'

'I find it difficult to believe that either brother would kill their golden goose, Sir.'

'I tend to agree; although I have a feeling the motive for Jennings' murder was probably not financial.'

Do you think it could have been a revenge killing?

'Possibly, but whatever the motive, it was an act that was charged with incredible emotion.'

'Is it too early to rule anybody out and concentrate on those that are left?'

'Well, let's look at what we know and what we can surmise,' Parrot said thoughtfully.

'Right,' replied Sweeney eagerly. 'Oliver Tapley has a motive. Jennings broke his nose and humiliated him.'

'It would have been a rather over the top reaction if, in fact, Jennings had punched him, but I should tell you that it was Julie Pattison who inflicted Tapley's injury.'

'Really, why didn't you tell me, Sir?'

'It was an unimportant piece of information until this morning, sergeant,' Parrot said to his young colleague without a trace of apology.

'What about John Tapley? He and Jennings did have that set to the other day.'

'I somehow just don't see John Tapley committing such a brutal crime over a dust up about the film running over budget, and it would only serve to suspend shooting, and the producers would lose a great deal more money,' Parrot said logically.

'What about Jane Warren, Sir? Jennings did ruin her best friend's life.'

'According to Jane, her friend is doing great…and why wait so long to take your revenge? No, that doesn't fit, but what if Julie Pattison was a good deal more upset than she let on. After all, we only have her word that their break up was mutual. What if he called it off and she was heartbroken? Then, a couple of weeks later, he starts to date Stephanie Scarll, and that and the rejection pushes her over the edge. Then, taking this supposition a stage further, suppose a desperate Julie had opened up to her mother and Sheila confronted Jennings in his trailer. Could be that Jennings, after consuming a bottle of red wine, was particularly dismissive to her, and offensive about Julie, which provoked her to pick up the letter opener and plunge it into him while his back was turned. Never underestimate the power of a mother's love or hate, Sweeney.'

'It's certainly an interesting theory, but Julie didn't seem the slightest bit bothered about Jennings, and she did tell me how relieved she was to be out of the relationship.'

'I'm sure she did, but keep in mind that she is a very good actress,' said Parrot, somewhat to the annoyance of his sergeant.

Changing the subject, Sweeney said, 'Jeremy Saville also has a motive. Apparently, Jennings had been giving him a rough time on the set and, according to Julie, had said that his acting ability was comparable to that of a tree stump: wooden, uninteresting, and unlikely to grow into anything substantial. So, being humiliated in front of a laughing camera crew may have provoked him enough to carry out the murder.'

'More than enough,' said Parrot. 'Humiliation is a strong motive, though judging from Jennings' record, I'd say there were a whole host of actors and film crew who fall into the same category.'

'What about Victoria and her family, Sir?'

'Let's leave them till after I've spoken to Peter Scarll. Now, I have to stand to attention as our venerable chief constable takes the stage, but, before I do that, consider another scenario of two people sharing a bottle of wine, when, suddenly, a violent argument erupts, leaving the director dead. The murderer removes the other claret glass and vanishes into the night to Lord knows where.'

Sweeney's demeanor suddenly changed, and Parrot said, 'Have I stirred some thoughts, sergeant?'

'Yes, Sir. Good quality claret is Julie Pattison's favorite drink. I never gave it a thought until your alternative view of events just then.'

'Understandable, Daniel, but a detective inspector needs to explore every angle, no matter how unpalatable that may be, especially if the case is one of murder.'

'Yes, Sir, I understand, but it's difficult when you like someone. Have you never felt torn during an investigation?'

'Can't afford to be. This is a difficult profession we've chosen. If you can't detach your feelings, your ability to detect is compromised,' said Parrot, trying to look sanguine. 'Look, I'll be honest with you; I think Victoria Croft is a splendid person whom Audrey and I like very much. I don't think she killed Jennings, but I can't be positive, so I need to treat her as a potential suspect and ignore my emotions. Which, after all, should play no part in the detection of a crime, and, that, Sergeant, is a famous quote from none other than Mr Sherlock Holmes and addressed to Dr. John Watson,' said Parrot with a nod of the head, before making his way to the dreaded press conference, which turned out as he expected: 'The Oswald Rowley Extravaganza' complete with assurances, affirmations, and platitudes, whilst Parrot had to stand by his side, trying his very best to appear professional and supportive, quite a feat in itself, given the gut-wrenching oratory that was being thrust on the assembled audience.

Parrot quickly made himself scarce as soon as Rowley invited questions from the press and caught up with Sweeney.

'Come on; let's interview Julie Pattison.'

'I thought you were going to question her alone, Sir?'

'Yes, I was, but I don't need to wrap you in cotton wool, do I, Sergeant?'

'No, Sir, you don't, and thank you,' Sweeney said gratefully.

They found Julie Pattison in her trailer. It was obvious that she had been crying. The two policemen sat down, and Parrot said quietly, 'I appreciate that you've had quite a shock, but I need to ask you some questions.'

'Yes, of course, what do you want to know?'

'When did you last see Charles Jennings?'

'I went to see him last night in his trailer, to ask his advice about a scene I was scheduled to shoot this morning.'

'What time was this?' asked Parrot.

'About ten thirty.'

'And how long did you stay?' Sweeney said a little too aggressively, thought Parrot.

'About half an hour. He gave me some pointers, and I left,' she said with a defiant look aimed at Sweeney.

'Had he been drinking before you got there Julie?' Parrot asked.

'Yes, there was a bottle of wine already opened on his desk.'

'Did you have a glass with him?'

'No. He offered, but I wanted to practice my lines for this morning, so I refused.'

'So you went back to your room at the Hall about eleven o'clock, right?'

'No, I went to my trailer and worked on the script for half an hour, got a glass of milk from the kitchen, and went back to my room and fell asleep straight away.'

'Did you see or speak to anyone else during that time?'

'Only Winifred. She was in the kitchen with cocoa and chocolate biscuits; she said that it was the only decadent thing she could think to do at her age.'

'Any news yet on the film's rescheduling?' asked a smiling Sweeney.

'I rang John Tapley earlier, and he's already been in contact with a top director who's familiar with the book and would jump at the chance to fill the breach. In the meantime, we've all been given a week off.'

'Maybe longer,' said Parrot. 'Remember, this whole area is now a major crime scene and will remain one until we find the person or persons responsible.'

A sharp knock on the trailer door halted proceedings. 'Excuse me, Sir,' came the loud voice of Constable Malcolm 'Spider' Webb, 'but the Tapley brothers have just arrived back.'

'Alright, Spider, no need to shout,' said Sweeney, emerging from the trailer.

'Do you want to interview them, Sir?'

'No, I'll leave them to you, Sergeant,' said Parrot. 'When you've finished, take statements from Rachel Croft and Jacob Scarll, then talk to the chap in the film crew who discovered the body. Oh, and take Webb with you and see he keeps out of trouble.'

'Where will you be, Sir?'

'I think it's about time I spoke to Steven Scarll; then, I'm going to the Forester's for a pint and a pie. Why don't the pair of you come with me? Let's meet up at around twelve forty-five.'

'Right you are, Sir. Come on, Constable, let's get cracking,' Sweeney said, then, out of Parrot's earshot, added, 'Hope you've got some money on you, Spider.'

The composer was sitting up in bed and admitted to Parrot that he was feeling a lot better.

'That's good. You obviously know that Charles Jennings has been murdered?'

'Yes, Victoria told me earlier…what a terrible business.'

'Have you left this room since you started to feel unwell?'

'No, Chief Inspector, I've only got out of bed a few times to go to the bathroom, and that was a bit of an effort.'

'I need to ask your feelings about Stephanie's liaison with Jennings.'

'Well, frankly, I was unhappy that she was seeing him.'

'Did you voice your objections to her?'

'I did, though it had little effect.'

'What exactly did you say?'

'I told her that he was unpleasant, unsuitable, and he was just using her.'

'What was her reaction?'

'Stephanie is a quiet girl, Mr Parrot; yet, she has a stubborn streak. Like me, she detests confrontation, so she placated the situation by telling me that he was just a friend and no more.'

'Did you believe her?'

'Unfortunately not, and I told her so. I probably overdid the concerned father approach. We ended up having our first ever blazing row.'

'When exactly did this row take place?'

'On Monday morning.'

'And have you raised the subject with her since, or with anyone else perhaps?'

'Not with Stephanie, but I spoke to my sister, who suggested that Rachel and Jacob should talk to her. Victoria thought that because the three of them were so close and of the same age, Stephanie would be more likely to take notice.'

'And did she?'

'I'm afraid not. In fact, she exploded at them to mind their own business before coming in here and telling me much the same.'

'When did all this take place?'

'Yesterday afternoon.'

'Have you spoken to Stephanie since then?'

'No. Victoria has asked her to come and see me, but, so far, nothing.'

'Give it time; she's obviously distressed by today's events,' said Parrot, trying to sound as sympathetic as possible. 'Now, is there anything else you think I should know?'

The composer shook his head. 'No, nothing springs to mind.'

'Very well,' said Parrot. 'I'll leave you in peace, and I'm glad to see you're feeling better.'

'Thank you, Mr Parrot, and thank you also for your kind consideration. Tell Audrey that I promise to play for her when she next visits.'

Parrot tracked down Sweeney and Webb. 'Right, you two, let's head to the pub. I need a pint.' They walked to the car, where Parrot got into the backseat, stretched out, and pulled a standard issue police blanket over himself.

'What's going on, Sir?' said Spider.

'Tell him, Sweeney,' said Parrot from underneath his cover.

'If the reporters at the front gate see the chief inspector in the car, they will follow us to the Forester's, so this way we can compare notes in peace over a pint while they remain occupied, right, Sir?'

'Right, Sergeant. Let's go.'

The uniformed officers at the front gate kept the press and the photographers far enough away from the police car to ensure that Parrot was not spotted. Five minutes later, he and Sweeney were enjoying a couple of pints of 'Trooper's Folly' in a quiet booth of the Forester's, while their seconded driver had to make do with orange juice.

'Anything of interest from your interviews this morning, Sweeney?' asked Parrot.

'Yes, Sir, one thing in particular, and it came about by sheer chance. I happened to ask the Tapleys about their weekend trip to London with Charles Jennings, and John Tapley told me that Jennings only spent a couple of hours with them on Saturday afternoon before leaving, saying he'd arranged to meet an old friend. Tapley said he really didn't understand why Jennings tagged along in the first place; it wasn't as though he was particularly interested in the publicity side of the film.'

'No,' said Parrot, 'but he was very interested in meeting Stephanie Scarll for the evening.'

'Exactly, Sir, and listen to this. I called the number Stephanie gave me for her school friend and spoke to a Mrs Vinnicombe, the girl's mother, who told me that Stephanie had arrived early Sunday afternoon and left around lunchtime on Monday.'

'Good work, Sergeant,' said Parrot enthusiastically.

'Wait, Sir, it gets better. I asked her if she had spoken to anybody at Hadleigh Hall, to which she replied that she had rang on Monday afternoon after driving Stephanie to the station, just to let them know that she was safely on the train and should be back home around three thirty.'

'Come on, Sweeney, who answered the phone?'

'Victoria Croft.'

'And was there a conversation between them?'

'There was, Sir, and Mrs Vinnicombe happened to mention that it was such a shame that Stephanie had missed the local village fair on Saturday afternoon.'

'Even better work, Sergeant. Now, I wonder who Victoria Croft shared that information with,' thought Parrot aloud.

'Maybe she kept quiet, Sir. You know, not to worry the family,' said Constable Webb.

'I think not, Constable. I don't think that it was co-incidental that her brother was suddenly taken unwell. I think it was a direct result of finding out from Victoria that his daughter's feelings for Jennings were a lot stronger than she was prepared to admit to the family. So strong that she deliberately misled them about her trip at the weekend.'

'Do you still think Victoria isn't the murderer, Sir?' said Sweeney.

'Oh, I'm pretty sure she didn't commit the murder, but I'm equally sure that it's tied up with the family and Stephanie's behavior over the last few days.'

'Do you suspect Peter Scarll, Sir?'

'No, I'm not a doctor, but he still looked pretty weak to me a couple of hours ago, and I doubt he had the strength to get from his bed to Jennings' trailer.'

'He could have been driven by anger and desperation,' said Webb.

'That's right,' Sweeney said. 'After all, to witness his devoted daughter's personality change in such a short space of time, to the point where she is berating and screaming at him for interfering must have been very difficult for him to cope with and gives him a strong motive for murder.'

'I can't fault your logic, Sergeant, but there's more to this case. I'm sure there is. Don't ask me what, but I'm convinced there is something we've yet to uncover.'

A new voice suddenly joined the conversation. 'Speaking of covers, Mr Parrot, that was a neat trick you pulled back there in the car,' said Mick Tilbury, chief crime reporter of one of the few remaining quality national newspapers.

'Evidently not neat enough,' said Parrot. 'I thought you were staying on for the chief constable's question and answer session?'

'Do me a favor, Mr Parrot; all that old windbag is good for is insomnia,' which instantly brought broad smiles to Webb and Sweeney's faces. 'No. I preferred to follow you three likely lads. From what I just heard, I made the right call.'

'There was no way you were trailing us,' said the constable.

'Didn't have to. As soon as I saw Mr Parrot leaving with the two of you after the briefing, it was just a matter of finding the right pub. The Foresters was fourth on my list.'

'Look, Mr Tilbury,' said Parrot, 'you know I can't discuss this case, so what do you want?'

'Just a slight edge, Mr Parrot, so the inside track, when you've cracked the nut, would be much appreciated.'

'I really don't know how this is going to pan out, and I may not be in a position to give you the inside track,' said Parrot seriously.

'Give me your word that you'll try. That's good enough for me,' said the reporter.

'I'll do my best, but I don't want to see anything in print about what you may just have overheard, or all bets are off.'

'I don't know what you're talking about, Chief Inspector. I didn't hear a word.' With a nod and a wave, Mick Tilbury left as suddenly as he'd arrived.'

'Who is that character, Sir?' said Sweeney. 'And why are you pandering to him?'

'Because we go back a long way. When I joined the force, we were stationed together. He was a detective sergeant. We hit it off straight away and became good friends. Then, I was his sergeant when he got his promotion to inspector. We worked together for a few years until my promotion. The boys at the station and some of the villains used to call us George and the Dragon because of Mick's fiery temper, but, most of the time, it was an act...you know, the old good cop, bad cop routine before it became passé. Anyway, after I moved here, we still kept in touch and would meet up occasionally. Then, one day, out of the blue about ten years ago, he appeared up on my doorstep and asked to stay for a few days. Turns out that he had got himself involved with a woman that everyone but he could see was a bad lot, but the poor bloke was smitten. Took him a while to come to his senses, but, in the meantime, it cost him his family and his job.'

'Did they kick him out of the force, Sir?' asked Sweeney.

'Early retirement, Sergeant, if you know what I mean. Unfortunately, he made some poor judgment calls in serious cases while his life was in turmoil, and the powers that be decided he was a high profile liability.'

'Did he save the marriage, Sir?' asked Webb.

'No, Constable; that ended in divorce, but at least he's on speaking terms now with his two kids.'

'One thing puzzles me...if you are such old friends, why do you call each other Mister?' asked Sweeney.

'Professional courtesy. Apart from being an honorable man, Mick would never presume on our friendship in front of strangers.'

'But he did ask you to give him an edge, Sir. I'd say that was presuming on your friendship,' Sweeney said with some force.

'Not at all. That's his business. Come on, Sergeant. Surely you don't need me to draw you a picture of how we operate with the press? Anyway, back to the matter in hand; when we get back to the Hall, I want to interview Victoria Croft, together with Peter and Stephanie Scarll. Let's use the library. I'm sure Peter Scarll is well enough to come downstairs, but, if you have any arguments from the family, I want you to be polite but insistent—bring him down in a wheelchair if necessary.'

'Where will you be, Sir?' asked Sweeney.

'Just around. I need you and Webb to set the stage for my entrance. So to that effect, I need you both to arrange this interview in as detached and businesslike way as possible. I want all three of them to feel ill at ease by the time I arrive, okay? Any questions?'

'Do you really think one of them killed Jennings?' asked Webb.

'I honestly don't know, but I'm hoping that if we can put enough pressure on them individually, we may flush out the one responsible.'

The three policemen drove back to the Hall, this time with Parrot sitting in the front passenger seat. He was aware that the encamped media outside the Hall, which had swollen in numbers since their ruse, now realized that they had been hoodwinked. A cry of 'Crafty old buggar' brought a smile to all three policemen's faces.'

Sweeney and Webb immediately set about following their chief inspector's instructions, and Parrot left to his own devices for a few minutes decided to call Harry Starkey.

'Hello, George, not much else to add, I'm afraid. I can narrow the time of death down to between eleven thirty and one o'clock, and he had a large amount of alcohol in his system. The murder weapon contained only the victims' prints, and as you can imagine, the trailer is smothered with prints from all and sundry, and we're still lifting them.'

'Thanks, Harry, catch you later. Oh, by the way, I bumped into Mick Tilbury just now, and I'm going to invite him round to my place for a drink this evening, why don't you and Sheila come over?'

'Love to, we haven't seen Mick for years. Smashing bloke; how's he doing?'

'He's fine,' said Parrot, then spotting the raised arm of Sergeant Sweeney, said, 'see you about seven then, Harry; got to dash.'

With Sweeney and Webb positioned in the library, Parrot entered the room with an emphasized gravitas. Looking at each of the suspects in a nondescript fashion as possible, he spoke in a measured tone. 'I've asked you here to be questioned in a group because of certain evidence that has come to light, which I believe is central to this enquiry. Evidence that has been withheld by each of you, for whatever reason, that has obstructed this investigation. I'll start with you Stephanie. You lied to me when you told me that Charles Jennings was just a friend. Or, as you put it, like an uncle. You lied to your family about spending the weekend with a school friend, when, in fact, you traveled to London to spend the night with this uncle figure of yours, with whom you had become totally infatuated. Furthermore, I think you lied to me when you said that you didn't kill him. I think you went to his trailer to be with him, but he had been drinking and became abusive and violent. I think you picked up the nearest thing to hand and plunged it into your lover's neck.'

'Stop it. Stop it. Stop it,' came the shrieking howls of anguish from Peter Scarll at watching his beloved daughter's contorted face filled with horror and hearing her intense, uncontrollable sobs as Parrot spoke.

'I killed him; it's me you want,' said the composer, with head bowed.

'No, you didn't, Mr Scarll. You were in no fit state to murder anyone, but you did know about your daughter's liaison with Jennings because you were told by your sister, am I right, Victoria?'

'Yes, I told Peter, and I wished to God that I hadn't. You know, we spend so much of our lives protecting those we love that we sometimes forget to let those people make their own mistakes, and I'm as guilty of that as anyone.'

'No, my dear, you're not guilty of anything, unless cherishing and protecting those close to us has suddenly become a crime,' said Winifred Creamer from the now opened doorway.

'I'm sorry, Winifred, but I really must ask you to leave, until I have finished my questioning,' said Parrot in an exasperated tone.

'You very nearly have, Chief Inspector,' she replied quietly, ignoring his demand and crossing the room, before sitting next to her goddaughter and gently taking hold of her hand.

'Very well, you can stay, but I must insist on no more interruptions, understood?'

'Understood, Mr Parrot, but forgive me if I may interrupt you one final time.'

'What is it then, Winifred?'

'Well, I thought you might like to know that it was little old me that drove the letter opener into that black-hearted bastard's neck.'

'Winnie, it's okay; there's no need for you to get involved in this mess,' said Victoria.

'But I'm deadly serious, my darling Vicky. I truly did kill him. Frankly, I feel no remorse, just a feeling that I've done the world a service. Quite shocking, isn't it?'

Parrot did look shocked, as did Sweeney and Webb, but there was no doubting the conviction in Winifred Creamer's confession…added to the fact that the letter opener was not public knowledge, it made Parrot act quickly.

'Victoria, would you, Steven, and Stephanie mind leaving the room while we question Winifred?'

'Please let me stay, George. She doesn't know what she's saying,' Victoria pleaded.

'You three cut along now. I'll be just fine and dandy,' said Winifred, easing Parrot's predicament.

'It's for the best, Victoria. You can see her shortly,' Parrot said softly.

Parrot stationed Constable Webb outside the library door and told him not to allow anyone into the room for the next fifteen minutes. Both Parrot and Sweeney sat down, with Winifred Creamer between them.

'Now, Winifred, you have confessed to the murder of Charles Jennings, and it's my duty to caution you.'

'Yes, I know that, George, but tell me, is this interview official? You know, can it be used in court?'

'No, this is a preliminary, unrecorded interview. If we do charge you, it will be at the interview room at Hadleigh Station, and any conversation there will be taped.'

'Good, let's get started, shall we?'

'We need to be quite sure that you are not confessing to protect someone.'

'Well, of course I am, George, but not in the way you mean it.'

'I'm sorry, you've lost me, Winifred, and I suspect Sergeant Sweeney, too. What do you mean?'

'I can hardly protect anyone from a murder that I actually committed, Chief Inspector, but I can protect my family from the circumstances leading up to the murder becoming public knowledge. So, if both of you agree, I will tell you now exactly what happened last night. Providing you accept a slightly different version when you officially charge me later.'

'This is very irregular, Winifred. I'm not sure that we can go along with this.'

'In that case, I suggest you take me to the station right now and charge me.'

'Wait a minute, Sergeant, go keep Constable Webb company, will you? And don't come back until I call you,' Parrot said to a disappointed-looking Sweeney, who nevertheless quickly made himself scarce.

'Right, Winifred, this is now a private conversation with no witnesses, so please feel free to tell me what happened last night.'

'Right you are, George. Well, you are already mostly aware of what's been happening here for the past week or so, and the effect it's had on my beloved family. I feel responsible, because it was I that suggested the Hall as a perfect location for the film. If not for that, Stephanie would never have fallen under the spell of that evil man. I went to his trailer at around eleven thirty after I spoke to Julie Pattison in the kitchen. She had told me that he was still working on this morning's shoot. I thought that I could explain to him that he was causing the family enormous pain, especially to Steven who has been literally sick with worry. I should have saved my breath.'

'Was he drunk?' asked Parrot.

'As a skunk, but that was no excuse for what he said.'

'And what did he say that made you stab him?'

'Well, I realized that he was in a belligerent mood when I knocked on the trailer door. He said, 'Whoever that is, I'm bloody busy, so you can bloody well clear off. I substitute bloody for something more profane, George.

'This made Parrot smile. 'Understood.'

'Anyway,' continued Winifred, 'I wasn't going to be put off, so I went in. When he saw me, he said, "Oh no, what the bloody hell do you want?" I told him that his relationship with Stephanie was causing us all untold grief and asked him to stop seeing her. He laughed in such a horrible way, and then said, "Stop seeing her? You must be bloody mad, you old hag. When I'm finished here, I'm going to her room, and then I intend to screw the arse off the dirty little bitch. Now get the hell out of my bloody face, you dried up old bag." He swiveled round in his chair, so that his back was towards me. Then I saw what I thought was a small knife on the desk. I picked it up and plunged it into the back of his neck with all the force I could muster. And you know, George, it all felt incredibly surreal. Ten minutes earlier, I'd been drinking cocoa and thinking about going to bed; then, all of a sudden, I'm standing over a dead man's body, very strange experience. I did have the presence of mind, though, to thoroughly wipe the handle of the letter opener with a handkerchief, before going to my room, where I slept surprisingly well. And there you have the true story.

'The version I will be giving you at the station, however, will have no references to any member of my family and will center solely around my late night visit to the director's trailer to voice my concern over his treatment of my screenplay and his subsequent torrent of vitriol.'

'You know that the true story is far more likely to get you a shorter sentence because of the excessive provocation,' Parrot said.

'Not a concern of mine, George. My only concern now is to protect my family.'

'You know that they wouldn't want you to go through with this if they knew the truth, don't you, Winifred?'

'I'm aware of that, but you're not going to tell them, are you, George?'

'Not if you don't want me to, but I have to tell you that you are making too big a sacrifice.'

'Good lad, I'd a feeling I could count on you. Please call me Winnie...all my family and friends call me Winnie,' she said, smiling contentedly at Parrot.

'You mentioned that your families had been close friends for generations, Winnie.'

'Yes, that's right, for nearly seventy years.'

PARROT & SWEENEY

'Sometimes a little more than close friend's maybe?' probed Parrot.

'Could be, Chief Inspector "Smarty Pants" Parrot... go on, you're just itching to ask me something, aren't you?' she said, laughing.

'I couldn't help noticing the facial similarities between you and Peter Scarll.'

'Between us again, George?'

Yes, between us again, Winnie.'

'My father was a wonderful man, George, but his weakness was a roving eye. Well, one particular day, it roved over Lydia Scarll and hello Peter. My father confessed to my mother on his deathbed, and she in turn told me on hers. It was strange and wonderful at nearly fifty years of age to find I had a brother and a niece, both of whom I already considered as family.'

'Are Steven and Victoria aware?'

'No, I decided to carry on the Creamer tradition and tell them just before I kick the bucket,' she said, laughing even more heartily this time.

'I'd be lying to you, Winnie, if I told you that this is an easy burden for me to carry; frankly, the thought of you spending unnecessary time in prison appalls me.'

'Look, George, I don't want you to lose any sleep over this. I'm going to go through with this no matter what, with no doubts, fears, or reservations, and with total peace of mind. Family and friends come first, George, every time. Audrey tells me that you have two beautiful daughters whom you both adore. Well, put yourself in a position where you could spare them the stigma of public pain and suffering by suffering a little yourself.

My money say's that Audrey and you would fight each other for the right to protect them. Family and friends, George, most important part of our lives.'

'I'm not going to try to persuade you anymore, Winnie, but I would like to say that it is a privilege to know you, and I'll do everything in my power to see you get as light a sentence as possible.'

'I appreciate that, George Parrot. It's good to know there are honorable people roaming our planet. On that note, I suppose you had better take me to the station.'

Parrot called Sweeney and Webb back into the library and said, 'Right, you two, I want you to escort Ms Creamer to the station and charge her with the murder of Charles Jennings. I'll be there in half an hour to take her statement. Bring the van with the blackened windows to the rear of the Hall; then, drive to the rear entrance of the station. I don't want the media seeing her. So alert uniform at the front gate to form a cordon to prevent them from getting near to the vehicle, understood?' said Parrot, firmly.

'Yes, Sir,' both men said in hushed tones.

As soon as Winifred was on her way, Parrot made a couple of phone calls, and then asked Victoria to come into the library. He told her about her godmother's arrest. When she asked what exactly had happened the previous night, he gave her a potted version of Winifred's number two account. She then left to tell the rest of the family, and Parrot hurried along to inform Chief Constable Rowley of Winifred Creamer's arrest.'

'Are you absolutely sure about this, Parrot?' he asked, a shade disappointedly, Parrot thought.

'Positive, Sir. We have a confession, and I'm on my way to the station to take her statement. Is everything alright, Sir?'

'Yes, it's just that I didn't expect you to solve the case so expediently, Chief Inspector, but very well done, first class work.'

'Well, you did say that you wanted a quick result, Sir. In that respect, I would like to commend Sergeant Sweeney for his excellent contribution that led directly to the arrest.'

'Yes, of course, good man Sweeney, young and bright, just what the force needs. I'll speak to him later. Well, congratulations again, Parrot. I'd better organize another press conference. Shame in a way that it's all over so soon, what with all these journalist chaps on their way here from all over the world. Still can't be helped…let me have a full report A.S.A.P.'

Parrot quickly understood that his boss had mentally factored in a sustained spell in the limelight, which would account for his somewhat less than joyous reaction to the arrest.

That evening, George and Audrey Parrot and their guests, Harry and Sheila Starkey, Mick Tilbury, and Daniel Sweeney, were enjoying a delicious Indian takeaway meal, when George raised his glass and proposed a toast to 'family and friends, the most important thing in life,' which was soundly echoed by everyone present. When he went to the kitchen for another bottle of wine, he was followed by Mick Tilbury. 'Thanks for the phone call, George, much appreciated. Anything I can do for you or Audrey, anytime, just ask.'

'Well, you know, Mick, I might just take you up on that offer, but, in the meantime, you might consider visiting us more often, and you can bring your new partner down to meet us you know. 'That's a promise, George, that I'm more than happy to keep.'

Later that evening, when they were alone. Audrey turned to her husband. 'I can't help thinking about Winifred.'

'It's Winnie; she likes her friends to call her Winnie.'

'I'm going to visit her in prison; you don't mind, do you, George?'

'Mind? I'll be coming with you. She's the most courageous and honorable person I think I've ever met, and I wish she was my godmother. Are you going to keep in touch with Victoria?'

'Definitely. She's going to need friends more than ever now.'

'Good. I'm pleased. Rowley still wants Sweeney and I to continue our visits to the Hall until the film is finished. He said, "You never know with these temperamental artistes, George; it wouldn't surprise me if we got another murder or two before they leave."'

Audrey burst out laughing. 'I think the wish is father to the thought, don't you, George?' at which they both laughed heartily.

PS.

Four months later, Winifred Creamer was sentenced to four years in prison for the murder of Charles

Jennings. The judge said that, although she had committed the most serious of crimes, he had taken into account the extreme provocation that she faced that night, and the medical evidence of the victim's drunken state and the testimony of the many witnesses who had come forward to corroborate his previous appalling behavior, when under the influence of alcohol. He said that the term should be spent at an open prison with the possibility of day and weekend release after one year of the sentence was served. The press warmly welcomed the leniency of the sentence, none more so than Mick Tilbury's newspaper, which had run a vigorous support campaign for the author during her trial. This had, in turn, been surreptitiously orchestrated by a certain senior police officer.

CPSIA information can be obtained at www.ICGtesting.com
Printed in the USA
BVOW021451220512

290838BV00010B/18/P